SOME
BY VIRTUE
FALL

THE SEVEN GODS:
BOOK ONE

SOME
BY VIRTUE
FALL

THE SEVEN GODS:
BOOK ONE

ALEXANDRA ROWLAND

This is a work of fiction. All of the characters, organizations, and events portrayed in this book are either products of the author's imagination or are used fictitiously.

ISBN: 978-1-957461-00-7

www.alexandrarowland.net

First edition, 2022.

ALSO BY ALEXANDRA ROWLAND

The Histories Of Arthwend and the Wide World

The Tales of the Chants:

A Conspiracy of Truths

A Choir of Lies

Over All the Earth (forthcoming)

The Seven Gods Series:

Some by Virtue Fall

A Taste of Gold and Iron (forthcoming)

Other Works

In the End

Finding Faeries

Uncollected Essays:

"In Our Own Image: Radical Empathy, Trickster Gods, and the
Importance of Being Irritating"

For Victoria,
Talesyn-favored.

SOME BY VIRTUE FALL

"I *wish* that we had Enryn!" Alvana said for what must have been the hundredth time. Saba had rather lost count after the first hour.

"We've got it down to three: Lisbeth, Nevenna, and whatshername. Make a choice." Saba sat back and crossed her arms.

"I *wish* that we had Enryn!"

"Well, we don't." They'd been at this for *two hours* already. Lunchtime had come and gone. "We have these three. Attend!"

She watched Alvana drag herself back to the table, pick up the page of scribbled notes, put it down, sigh, and pick it up again, holding it up to the thin, watery light streaming through the drafty window. "I can't remember which was which."

"Lisbeth Hunter. Blond, gorgeous tits; read Pompolo's monologue from *Thera and Kliode*."

"Mmm," said Alvana. "She's too... not Enryn."

"Whatshername, Iracena something-or-other. Fake name, obviously trying too hard. Chestnut hair, decent tits—"

"Enough about their tits!"

9

"Can't help it—decent tits, pretty eyes, a fiery reading of the aubade from *Annan and the Sea Nymph*, knows some swordplay."

"She's the one that had the snobby accent, right?"

"The *clearly fake* snobby accent, yes. Lastly, Nevenna Playne—tall, curly hair, smelled of cinnamon and cardamom. Her parents own that bakery on Trifle Street, I believe. Nearly made me cry with Caelavius's death scene, which I haven't done for... what, a decade? Fuck, has it been that long? Lady of Time have mercy."

"I notice you don't have a comment on her tits," Alvana said darkly.

"Wasn't anything to comment on, was there?"

Alvana sighed and dropped her head to the table. "I just want Enryn."

Saba prayed for patience. "We cannot have him," she said, enunciating carefully. "He's in prison. Even if he weren't, we couldn't cast him unless you wanted him arrested and us, fined. We have," she rapped on the page, "Nevenna Playne, Iracena whosits, Lisbeth Hunter."

"They're not right for it." Alvana sat up. "D'you think we could fit Enryn into some sort of disguise—"

Saba's laugh was half-snarl. "You want to break him out of prison and disguise him as a woman so that he can play a man? Our Enryn? Over six feet tall, thirty stone if he's a pound? Half of that is belly and the other half is beard? Can't even whisper without the windows rattling? *That* Enryn?"

Alvana propped her chin on her hand, grumbling at the notes. "Not her," she said at last, pointing to Lisbeth's name.

"I hear what you're saying, but I'd just like to point out: Gorgeous tits."

"I don't *care* about her tits!"

"Oh, *please*! Liar."

"She's not right for the part!"

"Fine." Saba inked the quill and struck a bold line through Lisbeth's name. "Iracena or Nevenna?" A long silence while Alvana chewed her lip at the page. "Flip a coin if you have to."

"Nevenna."

"Iracena can fence."

"Nevenna. Her Caelavius nearly made you cry."

"It did do that. All right, then. Nevenna." Good. Good to have that settled.

"I *want* Enryn for it," Alvana said.

"So do I. Hell, Enryn would want Enryn for it. Tough luck. Nevenna will have to do." Saba would *make* her do, if it came to that. She stretched hugely and ruffled her hands through her wiry curls.

"Do you think she can do it?"

"Sure."

"She made you cry."

"So we have established."

"With *Caelavius*."

"Indeed."

"Maybe Iracena is better. She can fence."

"You picked Nevenna."

"Maybe we should think about Iracena again."

"If you like her that much, we can find a part for her. Prince Leonor?"

"No, I want Lutha for that."

"Leonor's cousin, then."

"Then we could move Mabeth to play Felix, freeing up Katre for a swing. She's good as a swing."

"The best."

Alvana sighed. "All right."

"Is that it?"

"That's it."

Saba smiled. "Took us long enough. I'll write up the list and take it to the theater. See if I can get past the ravening hordes without being torn to pieces. Tomorrow, eight o'clock, remember."

Alvana nodded absently. "We'll be fine, won't we?"

"Yes. By the boards and backdrops, I swear it," Saba said firmly. "We're still afloat. For now."

"Barely."

$\sim$

Saba stalked across the wide cobblestone forecourt and under the ornate arch of brass lanterns which gave the Theater of Lights its name, shouldering her way through the anxious crowd of would-be players wringing their hands at the door. She said nothing to them, drew no attention to herself, made no proclamations about who she was or what business she had.

When she made it to the door, she took a small hammer and two tacks from her pocket. A silence rippled out slowly behind her.

She withdrew the page that she'd tucked into her doublet, slowly unfolded and examined it, holding it at just the wrong angle for anyone behind her to peek. She smoothed out a crease. Examined it again.

The tension behind her wound tighter with each moment she delayed.

She put the paper up against the door.

Paused.

Took it down again.

Someone in the crowd sobbed. Saba stifled a grin.

A tack at each corner and three taps had the page affixed to the door, carefully set into old holes where other tacks had held other casting sheets. Saba took her time stowing the hammer back into the deep pockets of her faintly threadbare simarre, a knee-length, sleeveless coat in the Pezian style.

She turned around, still blocking the page, and looked out over the tight-pressed crowd. Their eyes were so round and frightened, bless them. Some of them were crying. She raised her eyebrows and made a shooing motion at them; they scuffled to make a narrow path for her. She stuck her hands in the pockets of her coat, hopped off the front step, and sauntered through the crowd.

A scuffle erupted behind her as they all flung themselves towards the door at once.

There were men in the crowd. There had been some at the auditions too. Again and again, she and Alvana had explained to them the reasons why the troupe could do no more than listen politely to their auditions.

It was the same reason they couldn't have Enryn anymore. Or Dafyd, for that matter, or any of the others.

Once she'd made it across the forecourt, Saba turned to watch the carnage.

More tears. Most of the men were angry, of course, but that's what had gotten them banned from the stage in the first place. Between the duels and the riots, it was shocking that there were any left alive to *want* to perform.

"Pardon," said a voice like cream. A chill went down Saba's spine; she turned so quickly that she nearly lost her hat. "Aren't you Sabajan Hollant?"

"Aye," she said, already breathless. The woman standing before her was dressed in the colorful, airy style of Manghar-Khagra—her dress fit deliciously close about her breasts and torso without stays, flaring from her hips to a generously-cut skirt. The fabric—linen, woven in narrow vertical stripes of green and white—hung in heavy, straight folds to her ankles. Pewter buttons ran from neckline to knee; the lower half were open, showing a walnut-brown underskirt. Her sleeves were unbuttoned to the elbow, leaving her forearms bare—her skin was dark bronze, the color of oiled teak, only a few shades lighter than Saba's own rich brown and of a warmer tone; her hair was black and glossy; her eyes, the startling color of unexpected spring.

Saba whipped off her hat and bowed. "At your service, my lady. Er. Miss. Madam?" Curse her for a fool! One glance from this beauty and she was fumbling. "Pardon," she said. "My attention was occupied." She waved vaguely towards the theater.

The beauty smiled; Saba nearly swooned. "Announcing your new recruits?" Despite her foreign dress, her accent was pure Avaren—*so* local, in fact, that Saba could pinpoint nearly to the *street* where this goddess had spent her childhood. Somewhere near the south-center of the city, a bit off from the Shrine Bridge area, east of Mathenge and north of the Velvets. And oh, that voice—like cream, yes. Cream and honey in a golden bowl.

"Recruits, at long last, yes. I'm sorry, your name...?"

"Nazeya mes Akhal."

The name rang a very faint bell. "A player?"

"Not one so accomplished as you. I've often hoped to make your acquaintance." She extended her hand for Saba to shake.

These lines, at least, Saba had run a thousand times: She caught up Nazeya's hand and kissed the backs of her fingers. "The pleasure, I assure you, is entirely mine."

To Saba's delight, Nazeya let their hands linger together for a moment before she withdrew. "Congratulations on your return," she said. "Three months' prohibition, wasn't it, same as ours? The city has been so dark without you Lights."

"Ah, we're the Lord Chancellor's Players now," Saba said, attempting to puff some pride into her voice, though the admission weighed as heavy as sandbags. "Have been for a couple years now." And a long and tedious couple of years it had been, too—bowing and scraping to a patron had seemed like a good idea at the time. Less so now.

"Surely you're only the Lord Chancellor's on your play-bills and draper's receipts. To the common folk, you're a Light and always will be."

Saba could have kissed her just for that. She could have been a crone—hells, she could have been a *man*, and Saba would have kissed her for that.

"Anyway," Nazeya continued. "I wished only to greet you and express my pleasure at seeing the Theater of Lights with some life around it again. I don't mean to keep you. You must have important things to attend to."

Saba longed to say, *no, of course not, none whatsoever.* But it would not do to feign idleness to a lovely woman. They didn't like that sort of thing at all. "You know how it is."

"I do."

"I hope," said Saba before she could help herself, "I hope you'll be coming to see our performances? We'll have an old play tomorrow, and a new one very soon."

"But of course. Who would miss the opportunity to see the great Sabajan Hollant on the boards again at long last?"

"And you?" Saba said. "Was your troupe under the prohibition as well?"

"Yes." Nazeya winced. "We dragged ourselves out to the country to escape the... you know."

"The 'for six months, none of the listed troupes can perform within a day's ride of the city walls' bit?"

"Indeed. But we've been rehearsing at our patron's estate for the last week. We return tomorrow—a new play."

"I'll have to come see you sometime."

Nazeya's skin was too dark to show much of a blush, but she ducked her head and her smile was obviously pleased. "I'll be honored to have you in the audience. Good day, Mistress Hollant."

"Good day, Miss mes Akhal."

Nazeya swept by; Saba couldn't help but watch her go. As soon as the beauty had passed out of sight, Saba's slumped back against the wall and let out a long breath.

Well! She crammed her hat back onto her head. *Well!*

The burgeoning flush of infatuation froze and withered on the vine. "Oh, *fuck* me," Saba snarled. She'd forgotten to ask the woman *which* troupe she was with.

Shit. Perhaps someone knew her? Surely a beauty like that commanded everyone's attention. On the other hand, there were dozens of troupes in the city...

She sighed heavily and shoved her hands back in her pockets. There was a coffeehouse not too far away; she'd wait there for an hour until the ruckus around the theater abated, and then she'd return and make sure everything was prepared for tomorrow.

Tomorrow. At last.

The following dawn, Saba paid the coffeehouse on the corner a full princess to deliver pots of Zebidian light roast to the theater's yard at regular intervals—an extremely necessary expense.

The Theater of Lights was built according to Brassing-on-Abona's local standard: a stacked ring of galleries surrounding the central yard and the stage, which were open to the sky and the light but for the partial roof—the heavens—that hung over the stage, supported by two brightly-painted pillars. In the very center of the yard, Saba had set two chairs, a little table, a large bottle of ink, enough quills to feather an entire flock of geese, and the first coffee delivery.

She unbuckled her belt, flung off her simarre and her doublet, kicked off her shoes, peeled off her stockings, and dug her toes into the fresh, clean sawdust. It was still and quiet, a deliciously cool morning in early summer. Saba, in her shirt-sleeves and breeches with a fresh pot of coffee and the theater all to herself, was perfectly content.

Then the players began to arrive—only the new ones, of course. Only they would be so punctual.

Some of them tried to *greet* her. Though every one of them was taller than her, she stared them down until they slunk across the yard and stood in a nervous little knot, whispering amongst themselves.

The clocktower rang eight. Saba stood up, quaffed the rest of her coffee, and hooked her thumbs into the waistband of her breeches. "All right, *attend to me!*" Her voice echoed off the empty galleries. The newcomers snapped to attention. "I suppose it's time for us to get to know each other." She let the last few words drip with poison. It was important for baby players to know their place. Took some of the fight out of 'em. "As you are standing in what we can loosely consider to be *my theater*, I assume you know who I am. If by some amazing coincidence you don't, I'm Sabajan Hollant. You may, I suppose, call me Saba. Henceforth, I'm your mother, I'm your father, I'm your general and your priest. Most importantly," and she let the pause stretch out to its breaking point, "I'm your *director*.

"The play, as you know," she said, pacing slowly around the yard, "is a new one by our esteemed writer, Alvana Still-grail. It has everything that everyone likes best in a play—true love, wicked betrayal, good death monologues, a mad king, the Lord of Temptation... It is a very good play; I expect *you* to make it *great*." She flung a dagger of a glance at them; they all nodded furiously. "If you haven't been living under a rock for the last year, you know that by the King's Edict, men are banned from performing on stage. Some of you are going to have to get comfortable in britches." She wiggled her hips at them—a less crude way of implying *cock* than an outright thrust—and bestowed upon them one faint smile.

'Right! To the casting! Our heroine, Cosima, will be the astoundingly beautiful Artagne Grey, who is not here yet. *She* is a shareholder in the company and does not have to show up for these preliminary speeches, having had them tattooed on the insides of her eyelids years ago. Are any of *you* shareholders? No, you are not. Thus, you'll be on time every day, and we won't have any trouble in this little family.

'Our hero, Aucien, will be the *very* lucky newcomer, Nevenna Playne." Saba spared the girl a brief nod. 'This is an incredible opportunity for you. Don't fuck it up. We have another shareholder, Lutha Brewer, playing Cosima's lady-in-waiting. Mabeth Thatcher, a shareholder, as Piero, Cosima's brother. Iracena du Cassa as Orchilo, Aucien's cousin!" No one had perked up when she'd said that last name. 'Where's Iracena?"

No one spoke. Saba let her expression slowly freeze over.

'I see. In case you're wondering, Iracena is *not* a shareholder." Another silence stretched to the breaking point. 'Inneo Selwyne, shareholder, the soothsayer; Ishmeta and Talsyn Bhargava, shareholders, the queen and king, respectively. I'm the Lord of Temptation. You may notice that most of you haven't been named. There are a few more small speaking roles to fill and many bit parts. If there's anything you can do that you didn't mention in auditions—dancing, singing, stage-fighting, et cetera—do let us know about it."

The door creaked open and a girl with passable tits entered —ah, Iracena. And not even an ounce of shame showing.

'Good morning," Saba said warmly. 'Rehearsal starts promptly at eight."

'Yes, I know." Iracena glanced about at the others. 'Something wrong?"

'Is it eight o'clock now?" said Saba.

"As far as I know." Iracena was still using the terrible fake accent, trying to pass for snobbier than she was. Probably thought she was better than other people—Saba couldn't stand her sort.

Saba smiled sweetly. "It is, in fact, fast approaching fifteen minutes past. You've already missed the important announcements."

"Could you repeat them?"

"No."

Iracena frowned. "Why not?"

"Because rehearsal starts at eight." Dropping her honeyed tones: "You missed hearing what *part* you were assigned."

"I'm only a little late, I couldn't get out of the house—"

"A little late? Ten minutes late." Saba stalked up to her. "Can you imagine being ten minutes late to take your bows? You'd be bowing to an empty theater, chickadee." Iracena was taller than her by at least a handspan—nearly everyone was. Saba had long ago learned how to *act* tall. She could loom over someone from a seat on the floor if she wanted. "Your cue to enter the theater is the first toll of the eight o'clock bell. If you're not here by the time the echoes fade, you can find yourself a different company. Understood?"

Iracena went scarlet. "Now see here!"

"*Are we understood, Miss du Cassa?*" Silly, pompous name to go with the fake accent—she wasn't even Pezian, but obviously as Avaren as Saba herself.

"Yes," Iracena said tightly.

"You'd better thank me for giving you another chance."

"Your generosity knows no bounds."

"You're very welcome."

A little kerfuffle on the first day was a great gift in the long run. Now they all had the fear of god in them, or at the very least the fear of Saba.

Saba had little faith that the newcomers would able to find their own asses in the dark, so she began by drilling them on posturing and projection. Alvana arrived just before nine as Saba shrieked for the hundredth time, "Nevenna, pro*ject!*"

"How are they?" Alvana asked breathlessly, dropping a bundle of papers onto the table.

"Meh."

"Coffee?"

"Help yourself. These the scripts?" Saba pulled them over and flicked through; Alvana stole her coffee cup. "Nevvy, sweetheart, *project!*" she howled. "I'm a deaf blacksmith at the back of the yard, and my pockets are *full* of aging vegetables!" She dropped her voice. "How many?"

"Three copies," Alvana said, falling into her chair. "We're not having another repeat of last year."

"Good thinking. *Better*, Nevvy, thank you! Ladies, we have scripts, and I have rules for you about them."

"*More* rules?" said Iracena.

Alvana made a noise of surprise. "Goodness, who's that?"

"The queen of Vinte, apparently," Saba muttered. "Better known as Iracena."

"Who?"

"Our Orchilo." Partly to show Nevvy how it was done, Saba projected, "Yes, more rules. They're even more important than the rules about punctuality." She held the scripts high above her head. "The scripts, ladies! Three copies, which Alvana has painstakingly copied out in her own hand. Only three, so we'll be sharing them. You will not take them home with you, and you will *not* discuss their contents with anyone outside this troupe."

"If anyone asks what it is about," Alvana said, "tell them to come see the play and find out."

"Even if it's a small question, like—"

"Comedy or tragedy?"

"Or is it a history?"

"Do you think it's good?"

"What are the costumes like?"

"What role is Sabajan Hollant playing?"

"I don't care if it's your old granny asking on her deathbed, and I don't care if someone has a knife to your lover's throat: You say..." Saba gave them an expectant look, cupping her hand to her ear.

"Come see the play and find out," came the response, slow and scattered.

"Again!" Saba bellowed.

"Come see the play and find out."

"Louder!"

"Come see the play and find out!"

"Good! Now, we will be counting the scripts at the end of every day—"

"And probably at several points during the day," Alvana added.

"And then they go home with me or Alvana. If we could padlock them to our bodies, we would."

"So we don't get to take them home... ever," said Iracena.

Saba pasted a brilliant smile to her face. "I'm so glad you've followed the conversation."

"But how will we learn our lines?"

"You'll do your very fucking best, chickadee, right there on stage in rehearsal."

"If you're worried about them getting lost, why not print lots of copies?"

Saba dropped her face into her hands and screamed.

"It's not so much that we're concerned about *misplacing* the scripts," Alvana said, as Saba flung herself into her chair and grabbed wildly for their shared coffee cup. "More that they might be stolen. In a print shop, all the workers would see it; customers walking by might overhear the typesetter mumbling to herself. And perhaps one night the printer is balancing their accounts, and the earnings are looking a little scanty..."

"And a mysterious hooded figure appears in the doorway!" Saba said, gesticulating at an empty patch of air.

"The figure offers them money."

"A lot of money!"

"A *bag of money*."

"More than they've ever seen in their life!"

"And maybe their spouse is ill; maybe their daughter ran off with a philosopher."

"Maybe their cat exploded! There will be funeral costs!"

"And Maestre Printer thinks, what's the harm? All the figure wants is—"

They finished in unison: "A single copy of Alvana Still-grail's latest play."

"And then we're *fucked*," Saba finished.

"Explaining the script situation?" said a smoked-plums voice from the door.

"Hi, Artagne!" Saba said without looking around. "I love you! Run away with me."

"Can't, dear. Supposed to be in a play." Artagne stopped beside her, dropping a kiss atop her head. "I hear I've got the lead."

"Breaking my heart," Saba grunted. "Others?"

"Nearly here," Artagne said.

Saba smelled something, shot to her feet, seized Artagne's beautiful face, and sniffed her breath. "Beer. Why?"

"We stopped for a drink on the way over," Artagne said, giggling faintly. "To celebrate our glorious return."

"A drink."

"Well, three. Four, for some of us."

"Light of my eyes, queen of my heart, it is *nine in the morning.*"

"No, it isn't," Artagne said. The clock tower began to toll in the distance. "Well, now it is."

"Are the others as bad as you?"

"Mabeth stopped to throw up. The others are holding her hair back. I," Artagne swayed a little, "came ahead. So you wouldn't shout at us for being late."

"And now I'll shout at you for being staggering drunk!"

"I'm not drunk. I had... some drinks. Quickly."

"Why by all the gods did you drink three or four beers quickly before nine in the morning?"

"Didn't want to be late!" Artagne beamed at her.

The front door slammed open while Saba was still sputtering at her, and someone—Inneo—cried, "We're not late!" The remaining five shareholders wove their way across the yard, cackling amongst themselves like a flock of deeply inebriated hens. "Saba can't shout at us!" they sang. "We're not late! The clock just stopped ringing! We're not late!"

∼

"Right," Alvana said. "We'll start from the top, if everyone's not too drunk to read."

Alvana had wrested away control of the troupe. She and Saba had come to the "joint" decision that Saba would go up to the second story gallery and have a bit of a lie-down until the vein in her forehead stopped pulsing.

When Saba had collected enough of her composure that she was no longer in danger of exploding, she sat up and watched the players slurring and giggling their way through their lines as Alvana flitted between stage and table, muttering to herself and scribbling on the scripts.

The newcomers weren't *so* bad. Nevenna—Nevvy; she was

too young for Saba not to petname her, barely nineteen—was quiet and serious and lawyerish. Aucien would need some joy and boldness to him. Iracena had all the braggadocio and fire that Orchilo demanded, but she brought too much of herself on stage. The other newcomers were nothing spectacular yet, but they didn't need to be. The casting had only needed to fill in the cracks here and there.

The sun was peeking over the roof by the time they reached the grand entrance of Idunet, Lord of Temptation, the god of passion, greed, and hedonism—and the very best character in the play, in Saba's opinion. She already had visions of the costume she'd wear, the twisting figures of red and metallic gold she'd paint onto her dark skin until she burned and glittered like a creature of shadow and fire.

Saba stood on the gallery bench as Nevvy read Aucien's ritual of summoning; at her cue, she let her voice *boom* like thunder down to the stage.

"Who dares call me? Who dares to speak my name? What squirming mortal, blacken'd worm, what faint and trembling soul, milk-blooded, damp with piss?"

"Hold!" cried Alvana. "Everyone hold!" She put her hands on her hips, looking up to Saba looming above. "The hairs stood up on the back of my neck just then, Hollant."

Saba grinned. "Haven't lost my touch, eh?"

"Nothing close. Listen, I love having you there. For your entrance?"

"Here?"

"What do you think?"

"And fight my way through the groundlings to get to the stage? I? Sabajan Hollant?"

"We could fly you over."

"It'd ruin the surprise if I sat here with ropes tied to me for the first act. And it'd ruin the magic if I had to fumble them on and off in front of everyone. Also, half of the Lord of

24

Temptation is acted from the crotch." She thrust her pelvis to illustrate. "I'd prefer to walk it. But not through a few hundred screeching people."

"Can we rehearse it this way for now? Find a solution later?"

"As you like it."

"It's just that I was going to have you spring out from a trapdoor in the stage and—yes, yes, I know," she said when Saba grimaced.

"Trapdoors are beneath the Lord of Temptation's dignity."

"I'll concede that. D'you need a script?" Before Saba could even quirk an eyebrow, Alvana shook her head. "Don't know why I asked. Continue, Madam Hollant!"

"Do I need a script," Saba muttered. "Do I need a script! *Please.*" She rolled back her shoulders, widened her stance, acted from her crotch. "*Who dares!*"

There was a long silence.

"Nevvy, *project*," Alvana said. "Saba didn't even hear you."

"O Lord, magnificent and bright, 'tis I who speak your name. I, Aucien!"

The Lord of Temptation bristled. "What! You! The merest whelp! A pup of man! Just yesterday a babe in arms, in faith! You starveling would enchain Temptation's Lord, Dream-plucker, the Seductor of the World? I, who whisper into king's ears 'til their fingers twitch with greed and strain to raise their weapons or their wits to conquer what those twitching fingers seize? I, who turns a maiden's eye and plucks her purse until both weep?"

"No, Lord! I have an altogether different aim! In supplica-tion do I call to you."

"A supplication! Now I see! The whelp aspires to a liber-tine. How many battles hast thou fought, young whelp? I do not waste my gifts on untried swords. And tell me true, how many maiden's purses hast thou clutched? A supplication must demand some coin."

The theater door slammed open, and a voice thundered even louder than hers: "Sabajan Hollant, you're rattling the windows clear across the street!"

"Enryn!" Alvana squeaked, flying across the yard and into the first-floor gallery. Saba, jolted out of the Lord of Temptation, floundered wildly to the stairs.

Enryn caught Alvana in his enormous arms and lifted her clean off her feet. Saba flung herself at him—colliding with his side was much like colliding with that of a great bull. "You scoundrel, you cur!" she cried, throwing her arms around him as far as she could reach. "You've ruined all our lives and now you've come to sweep up the pieces, I suppose!"

Enryn set Alvana down and took Saba's hands. "Aye, Sabajan, my love, and to ask once again, trembling with hope as ever, if your position on menfolk has changed at all."

"I'll have nothing to do with the disgusting creatures! But as you're a scoundrel and a cur and not a man at all, you will hug me at *once*."

He laughed and swept her up too, squeezing until her spine crackled. By then, the other shareholders were likewise pounding up from the yard and tearfully flinging themselves on Enryn. Saba found herself set gently to the side while he engulfed each of them in turn. "I thought you weren't supposed to be out for another season!" Artagne said, standing on tiptoe to kiss Enryn soundly on his bristly cheek.

"I struck a deal," he said, returning her kiss threefold to both cheeks and her forehead. "I've been terribly well behaved, a perfect gentleman—" This made all of them snort, "—and I happened to save a guard's life when one of the other prisoners tried something stupid. Long story. Anyway, I asked for a favor and managed to come to an understanding with the Lord Warden. I'm to present myself at the prison twice a week and strictly avoid brawling of any kind. If I fail on either count," he added cheerfully, "then it's back in for another four months and I pay the Lord Warden three queens for his troubles."

"Only you could have talked someone 'round to a scheme like that," Saba said. "When did they let you out?"

"Just now. I came straight here." His expression grew sheepish. "If you weren't here, I was going to wait and twiddle my thumbs for as long as it took. Wasn't expecting the whole lot of you, though."

"Aha! A guilty conscience! I knew he'd try to avoid us!" Artagne said.

"No! I just... wanted to talk to Saba and Alvana first. I didn't know you were already rehearsing." His voice cracked on these last words. He looked over all their heads at the stage with a sudden desperate sadness that Saba recognized.

"You can talk to *me*," Saba said. "The others are quite busy getting over this morning's pub crawl."

Inneo snorted. "Oh please, it was one pub—"

"A pub crawl in that you crawled out of the pub," Saba snapped. "Away with you! Go rehearse! Enryn, with me." Lutha darted in to snatch another quick hug, which he bestowed with the greatest enthusiasm before following Saba up to her eyrie in the gallery. "I wasn't really rattling the windows across the street, was I?" she asked.

"Hah, not quite. I was only standing outside the door, trying to gather my courage to come inside, and I heard you declaiming. Couldn't make out the words, just your voice."

Saba straddled one of the benches. "Gathering courage? You didn't think we'd be angry with you, did you?" He shrugged. "Oh, sit down, you enormous fool. Have you ever known me to lie to you?"

"Only about whose turn it is to pay the bar tab."

"Damn right. So believe me when I say... I'm slightly miffed with you."

"Yes, I thought so," he said meekly, scrunching as small as such a huge man could.

"You and the others…" She rubbed her forehead. "It's not only *your* fault. It was a whole culture amongst you theater men. Amongst, hell, *all* you men. So there would've been some final straw eventually. Yet from another perspective, it is your fault, because you and the boys went to deal with shit yourselves instead of using the proper channels. *That* might have gotten us some justice. If you'd given Alvana time to get her papers in order…"

Somehow, he scrunched even smaller. "And now I can never stand on that stage again. Not me, not any of the others —not even Benji the draper's son. Little mite was begging to audition last summer. I told him ten wasn't old enough but that I'd hear him out if he came back in a couple years. I *promised.*"

They sat in somber silence for a moment. Below, Aucien traded pleas for barbs with the Lord of Temptation.

At length, Saba asked, "You wanted to talk about something?"

"I was wondering if you had anything I could do."

"Enryn."

"Please. Let me haul sawdust to floor the yard. Or scrub the galleries, or sell sausages to the groundlings, or build props. I'll learn to sew and make the costumes. I'll—hell, I'll stuff myself beneath the stage and crank the mechanisms."

Saba gazed down into the yard. "Don't know if that's allowed. I'll have to read the official document again."

"You don't already have it memorized?"

"Legal language isn't the same as Alvana's. But I've got most of it." She sighed heavily. "We were just going to make do ourselves, save some money. If it turns out we can't have men for the backstage staff either… I don't know if there are enough theater women in the whole city to supply us *and* every other troupe. We've abridged *The Shepherdess of Spring,* just to have something to perform today."

Enryn gave her a highly dubious look. "*Shepherdess?* Really?"

"Really and truly. We're working with the absolute minimum right now, and *Shepherdess* is forgiving like that— just bouncing, giggling, being lewd. No musicians or mechanisms required."

"It's not what I'd describe as a glorious and triumphant return for the Lights."

"No. But we need the coin."

"Fair enough. The smutty plays always draw a crowd. You heard anyone else's plans?"

She snorted. "The Lady Exchequer's Players claim they're doing ten wholly *new* plays this month. I'm simply *breathless* to see how that turns out."

"And the Lord Seneschal's Women?"

Saba couldn't help but hiss. "Speak not those words within these walls."

"Sorry. The Lord Slanderer's Gorgons, I meant. The Reds."

"Don't know. They've kept their traps shut for months. Hence why I wanted us to start as quickly as possible and get our foot in the door, even if it's trash like *Shepherdess.*"

"I saw someone hanging signs about their new play on my way over."

She snorted. "They must've found a new writer. We certainly haven't given them a chance to try any of their old tricks. We even retained a lawyer—Alvana took a copy of the play for him to keep safe, and we all signed a document, witnessed and notarized, so that we can prove that it was ours first if they try anything like last year."

"That's a wise precaution," Enryn rumbled.

"An *expensive* precaution. But he came with glowing recommendations. Wouldn't have trusted him, otherwise."

"Hah. You don't trust anyone but Alvana."

"Cruel and untrue. I trust you."

"Do you?"

"For most things, anyway. I trust you to keep secrets, and to have my back, and to be the greatest fun in bars and the best wingman I've ever had. I trusted you when we were on stage together. But I don't trust you anymore to keep your temper when your friends have been wronged. That's where I fucked up last year. I took my eyes off you boys for one goddamn second, and..." She gestured broadly. "Here we are."

"I'm sorry. Have I said that yet?"

"Don't think you have, no."

"I am."

"I'll be forgiving you soon." She gave him a wan smile. "I feel like I've thrown myself headlong off a cliff—either we plummet to our deaths, or the wind catches under our wings and we keep flying for another year. If we fly, then I'll be able to forgive you and mean it. If we fall... Likely I'll still forgive you, because I love you dearly, in spite of the fact that you're a damn fool wreck of a man. Not to mention a scoundrel and a cur." She took one of his hands in both of hers. "For now, I close my eyes and pray for the wind, and I have no attention to spare for forgiveness *or* condemnation."

He squeezed her hands. "If you can find some way for me to help..."

"I'll speak to the lawyer."

"I don't even need payment. Buy me a pint and I'll call that fair."

"And how do you expect to feed yourself that way? How do you expect to keep a roof over your head?"

"If I can't be in the theater, then it won't matter, because

I'll be dead and the only roof I'll have over my head will be the top of my casket."

'Oh, for heaven's sake, Enryn, stop it. If you really have to be on a proper stage, you could go somewhere else—Vinte, Bramandon, Heyrland. Or join a traveling company and tour in the country. The law only applies within a day's ride of Brassing's city walls."

'I can't leave. I wouldn't know what to do with myself anywhere else—I grew up here. Everyone I know is here, all my family." He gestured down to the yard, to the rest of the troupe.

'Half of your family has just been kicked out of their profession. They'll be looking for work too, as soon as they get out of prison. I'm sure they'd be happy to go with you." Saba laughed suddenly. 'You and the boys could start your very own touring troupe and stuff your bodices while we're here stuffing our breeches, and you could get up to all the brawling and licentious hedonism your little Idunet-loving hearts desire. Only one who'd mind that is Leony Token, right?"

"Token *is* terribly fond of his wife, that is true. Poor man just refuses to see the light and kneel in awe at the altar of cock. Anyone'd think *you'd* get along better with him." She snorted; he cast her a wry look. A moment later, he said neutrally, 'I see Tal's still here."

'Yes. What of it?"

'*He's* allowed to keep performing, is he?"

'Oh shit, we're not really going to have this vulgar conversation, are we?"

Enryn shrugged. 'I noticed, that's all. I don't begrudge him it. You're sure you won't get in trouble?"

'Hell if I know. Stupid wording in the Edict—they say *men* aren't allowed to perform, but they don't define what they consider a man to be. Do they think it's about what's in your trousers? We spent a few evenings wrestling with it, me and Tal and Maddie. We had long, ugly, wretched conversations about what might happen if the Master of the Revels had problems with the two of them."

'Fuck. Tal decided it was worth the risk?"

'He said if the Master of Revels decides it does come down to, ahem, *country matters*, he'll just drop trou and show his nothing, and His Lordship will have no choice but to relent. If His Lordship decides the other way, that it's about concept rather than cock, then Tal says he'll plead guilty, pay the fine for the company, and call it quits. We decided not to draw attention to ourselves by quibbling over semantics with the king's lawyers."

'And Maddie?"

'Maddie said she preferred her dignity, thanks, and gave her share to Tal—didn't sell it to him, *gave* it. She had a bit of money saved, so we threw her a party and away she went to Heyrland, since people are civilized there about the nuances of a person and she had contacts with a troupe in the capital. According to her last letter, she's got the lead in their new play and already has a little pack of shy, worshipful, universally adorable admirers who call her 'Beautiful Madagat'—alliterates in their language, apparently. She said to give you boys her love."

Enryn nodded glumly. 'I'm sorry to have missed seeing her off."

'Ugly, *ugly* situation. I hate that it's one more thing that she and Tal had to think about—especially because the theater was always the one place they *didn't* have to think about it—and I hate that Tal will have to weigh the risk every time we cast him. No good solutions except to let him and Maddie choose for themselves, and stand with Tal against the consequences if or when they occur, and send Maddie off with a grand party and all the love and pocket money we could pile on her. Nothing else we can do."

"There isn't, no." He sighed. "Thank you for talking to me."

"Dear creature, why wouldn't I talk to you?"

"I know I'm asking a lot of you—your time, your attention, your forgiveness. I'm afraid it must be tiresome of me." He winced. "No, that was clumsily said. Let me try again and make it a gift to you instead of self-flagellation: You're a good friend, Saba. It would break my heart to lose that friendship, and I'm unutterably thankful to find I haven't. I missed you every day, and I'm glad you're still here and still fighting."

Her eyes burned; she blinked the tears away and said airily, "Yes, tooth and nail. Don't know how to stop, really, and I wouldn't know what to do with myself if I managed it. Peace is an apoplexy." She clapped him on the shoulder. "You're a cur and a scoundrel but you've got the heart of a bear, for good and for ill. Why don't you stay for the afternoon? You can teach Nevvy to *fucking project*!" She bellowed this last at the stage. "And you can watch a lot of drunken women try to focus long enough to perform Alvana Stillgrail's latest masterpiece, *Some by Virtue Fall*."

Enryn went very, very still. Saba's blood was already running to ice when he said: "That's the title I saw on the Reds' posters."

~

Saba slammed back through the doors of the Theater of Lights, a torn poster in her fist, Enryn striding behind her with the power of a mountain in avalanche. "He was right," she thundered. "He was fucking right!"

Alvana, her fingernails now chewed to the quick, put her face in her hands and began to weep.

Saba crumpled the paper into a ball and flung it at the stage. "How?" she shouted. "How? *How?*"

Inneo dropped off the stage and went to embrace Alvana. Artagne picked up the crumpled poster and smoothed it out, as sober as a cold winter morning. "The Lord Seneschal's Women are pleased to announce a thrilling and heartbreaking new play by Zitka Yermekov and Verity Dauren, *Some by Virtue Fall*. A brilliant, tragic romance, to be shown in the Red Theater at two o'clock tomorrow afternoon, the seventeenth instant of Pasture-Month."

"They can't do that," Iracena said, snatching the poster away from Artagne, who merely raised her eyebrows.

"Damn right they can't!" Saba snarled. "We have proof! The lawyer!"

"Oh, for pity's sake, Saba," Alvana sobbed, wrenching herself out of Inneo's arms. "Who do you think gave it to them? No one else had a copy but him!"

"Who recommended him?" Saba demanded. "Do you remember?"

"No!" she wailed, gesturing hugely. "I mean, yes, but—it was several people! Everyone said he was trustworthy!"

Talsyn snorted. "Anyone remember that play Dauren wrote a couple years back? What was it called? *Gold and Greed* or something trite like that?"

"Ah," said Artagne, her voice growing even more frosty. "You're referring to the one where the villain pays off some drunkards to celebrate the trustworthiness of a certain priest where the hero can overhear."

"That's the one! But she's not a priest at all, the hero confesses everything to her, his plans are foiled, and it all comes to ruin."

Saba seized the coffeepot and flung it against the wall of the yard. It shattered, staining the sawdust and leaving gritty streaks of coffee-grounds down the paneling. "*Fuck*. We might as well have had it couriered straight to Yermekov by a cute little boy in livery!"

"Wait, wait," Inneo said. "Yes, there's the parallel with Dauren's play, but... Are you sure it was the lawyer? It's not unthinkable that the Reds could've gotten the script some other way—breaking into his office or Alvana's rooms, or going through her trash for drafts..."

"I never let a piece of paper cross my threshold unless it's bound up and held in my own hands!" Alvana's face had gone all splotchy red with tears. "I burn the rest. I won't make *that* mistake again!"

"Look, sobbing and smashing coffeepots isn't going to solve any problems," Inneo said.

"Are you not enraged?" Saba hissed. "Are you not *burning* right now?"

"Of course I am! If they've harmed us, I want them brought to justice, and properly this time. I want vengeance. But I want it to be precise and *permanent*."

"She's right," Iracena said.

"No one asked you!" Saba snarled. "You've been in this troupe for five minutes! What opinion could you *possibly* offer that would be relevant at this moment?"

"Don't speak to me like that. She's *right*. You should go to the authorities."

"Someone get this self-important little twit out of my theater," Saba said.

Iracena looked around at the others; no one would make eye contact with her. "Are you serious? I know people! I can help you with this!"

"Oh? You *know* people, do you, little girl? Who? Who do you know, with that fancy accent of yours that absolutely isn't fake in the slightest? Perhaps you're bosom friends with the Lord Seneschal's daughter? Perhaps the Master of Revels is a friend of the family and you grew up thinking of him as an uncle? Who, girl? Who do you *know*?" Iracena went scarlet and moved back, mumbling something inaudible. She dropped the poster—Saba dove across the yard, snatched it up, and tore it to shreds. 'I was already *planning* on taking it to the authorities. I'm not an idiot."

"We'll have to get another lawyer, if this one's turned on us. Or if he was never a lawyer to begin with," Artagne said as she gazed stonily down at the snowdrift of paper at Saba's feet. 'Saba can go see him; the rest should stay here and prepare for this afternoon's performance. Inneo's right—this has to be precise. No hotheaded men to charge in and get justice for themselves in bar-fights and street duels—we'll take the Reds to court, and we'll win. They'll have to wait another season to perform again, or they'll be disbanded, or imprisoned as thieves."

"But first, the lawyer," Saba said grimly.

He wasn't there. The landlady of the building went so far as to take Saba up the stairs and *show* her the empty room. When Saba pressed about what had become of the plain, thin, bearded gentleman, the landlady shrugged and said, 'He only rented it for three days."

Saba's gut clenched. 'But where did he go? What name did he give you? Profession? Has there been anyone else come to look for him? Did he say why he needed it for such a short time?"

After another few minutes of increasing agitation on Saba's part, the landlady lost her patience and showed Saba briskly out to the street.

No one else in the neighborhood even seemed to know who Saba meant, other than a sausage-seller down the street, and all *he* said was that the gentleman had bought lunch and supper from him not long ago, and that he'd seemed particularly cheerful on the last day, cheerful enough to for the sausage-seller to notice. "Must've come into some money, is what I thought!" the ancient man crowed. "Hared off to collect an inheritance from a long-lost uncle, I 'spect, like in one o' them plays!"

As he was the only person who had been any help at all, and as lunchtime had come and gone without her marking it, Saba bought a piping-hot sausage from the man and snarled her way back down the street.

A con artist. A *fucking* con artist in league with—or in the employ of—the Reds.

Those bitches wanted a war, did they? Part of Saba longed to give them one, to rush on them and consume them like a wildfire. Part of her, exhausted and defeated, longed for the good old days when the worst confrontation offered by a rival troupe was jibes traded in the taverns and back-alley scuffles that left no injuries more serious than bruised pride and blackened eyes.

This *malice aforethought*, this cold-blooded sabotage... This was new.

There was only one last place she could turn to for help: Their patron, the Lord Chancellor.

Oh, hateful man. Hateful man who did not understand theater life, who expected them to be a profitable business rather than scraping by year after year, paid half in coin and half in glory.

~

She wove her way through the tangled streets and crossed the river via Shrine Bridge, where she left the latter half of her sausage (which had burned her tongue rather badly) as an offering to Talesyn, the Lord of Players. "*Bro*," she said feelingly to the weatherworn likeness etched on the face of the enormous, ancient standing stone. "*Bro, come on.*"

That was all the prayer she could muster. Or that she had time for.

She ran the rest of the way.

The clerk in the entry hall of the Grand Chancery eyed her suspiciously as she charged through the doors. Wheezing for breath, she leaned on his desk and demanded, "Is the Lord Chancellor here? I need to talk to him."

"And who are you?"

"Sabajan Hollant, of the *Lord Chancellor's Players.*"

"Did he know you were coming?"

"Nope," Saba said. "But it's about the Reds—the Lord Seneschal's Players—so he'll want to see me."

"He's left for the day," the clerk said, folding his hands on the desk.

"Where to?"

"I'm not at liberty to divulge His Lordship's personal calendar."

"That's very much less than ideal." The clerk merely shrugged. "Listen, I have *very serious matters* to report. Our new play was stolen by our arch-rivals— "

"Arch-rivals?" the clerk asked, dry as the desert in summer.

"—Who are sponsored by, may I mention again, the Lord Seneschal. The play is Alvana Stillgrail's latest." At this, the clerk paused. "The Lord Chancellor will be extremely upset if he doesn't hear about this, and I'll tell him *you* were the one who kept the news from him. What's your name? So I don't have to describe you as *that smug, weaselly little shit at the desk.*"

The clerk glared. "You can write him a message if you like, and I'll have a runner take it to him."

"Fine."

The clerk set a sheet of paper in front of her with a flourish and, begrudgingly, allowed her access to his pen and inkpot. Saba scrawled out a few lines. "I cannot emphasize enough that this is a life-and-death matter."

"I'm sure it is."

"How much do I need to pay you to wipe off the smirk, eh?" Saba folded the paper with sharp movements. "I wasn't kidding about telling him it's your fault if the message doesn't reach him, my friend."

Another glare. "I'll take it to him myself," the clerk snarled. "And I'll put it into his own hand, if I can manage it. *Happy*?"

"Delighted."

Very early the next day, Saba looped through the theater district and edged past the garish walls of the Red Theater, which did *not* seem to have been conveniently closed for pest extermination or repairs. Perhaps the Lord Chancellor had other plans for them, then.

She was overtaken by a sudden fear, the sort of wilderness-panic that might have been sent by Wild Ystrac himself, and sprinted halfway across the city to the Chancery again. Even before she was through the door, the smug clerk at the desk snapped, "I did it, all right? Don't give me that look. I put it right into his hand!"

"Is he here? Can I talk to him? What did he say when he read it?"

"I don't know—he was busy, as I said. And," he added, "He's busy now."

"I just want to know what the plan is."

"I'm sure it's under control."

"Go in right now and tell him I'm here, and that I want to know what the plan is."

"He's with the *king*," the clerk said.

Saba paused, considered carefully.

The clerk sneered. "Are you as important as *the king*?"

A long, long silence while Saba continued considering. "No?"

"I'll remind him about your message when he gets out of his meeting. With," the clerk said crisply, once more, "the *king*."

Saba rubbed her hands over her face. "This matter is time sensitive. How long is the meeting likely to take?"

"I'm sure I couldn't say. But I'm thankful we have officials who take such care and consideration in the running of the country, don't you?"

"Oh, fuck off."

"I'll let his lordship know you stopped by, madam, but if you don't escort yourself out, then I'll see you *thrown* out."

∽

Well, there was nothing for it. Saba arranged for the other Lights to cover her part in that afternoon's performance and hied herself back to the Red Theater, where she lurked across the street and waited for the city watch to arrive by order of the Lord Chancellor and shut it all down.

By half past one, the forecourt was crammed full of theater-goers, and the girls at the door were taking pennies as fast as the flowing mass of humanity could hand them over.

Surely the watch would arrive, Saba thought. Probably any minute now. They were just waiting for a suitably dramatic moment—and oh, wasn't it worth a few pennies to get a better seat to see *that* performance?

She jostled through the crowd to the theater door. A penny to enter, then a split just inside: the sawdust-floored yard was for the groundlings, who'd pack in as tight as salted kippers; anyone wishing for a seat paid another penny for a spot on the benches of the first-floor gallery. Just as in Saba's own Theater of Lights, stairs led upwards to the higher galleries, each guarded by another attendant with another rattling box of coins.

Saba settled towards the back of the twopenny seats.

The authorities hadn't yet arrived by the time the play began.

Saba's manic tension wound tight through the brief invocation to Talesyn, Lord of Players—he who was named the Songspeaker, Clevertongue, Silverthroat, god of fire and music and the light of poetic inspiration, god of all that was known; he who was Saba's favorite above all other deities, who would surely, *surely* come through for her today of all days...

Her tension wound tighter as the play began, and tighter still through the first half of the first act, fading from the joy of revenge and vindication to impatience, then frustration, then the windchime-trembling of profoundly shaken expectations —what had happened to the message? Where was the watch to arrest these thieves and cheats?

Saba's world didn't end until Cosima's entrance.

Cosima, Alvana's latest and greatest heroine: a magnificent beauty famed throughout the land, but jinxed by fortune and unlucky in love. Artagne would've played her beautifully, bringing all the wistful regret, indefatigable hope, and delicate poignancy the role demanded until, at last, she died piteously and heart-rendingly in the third act.

But this Cosima. The Red's Cosima.

She was bronze-skinned where Artagne was fair. Her hair was glossy black, her wrists were delicate, and...

Saba knew her. The woman she'd met in front of the Theater of Lights. The beauty who had turned her head.

Nazeya mes Akhal. The one who had spoken to Saba in the street, who had greeted her by name and *flirted*, practically.

She was a Red.

No wonder she hadn't volunteered her troupe name.

Had Saba let something slip? Oh, Idunet curse her for a fool! She'd been so agog that she might've told Nazeya anything. She probably *would* have, if it had gotten her farther with that gorgeous creature.

And Yermekov knew that. She'd likely sent Nazeya deliberately. Saba would wager the takings from a week of performances on it.

So it was Saba's fault. She must have said *something* —about the play, about the lawyer.

Idunet, why? she mentally wailed. *What did I ever do to you? I was going to play you as having a huge dick! Lord of Temptation, why fuck with me like this?*

Even now, Saba couldn't take her eyes off Nazeya.

She *owned* the audience. She filled the theater from the sawdust in the yard to the rafters of the heavens, from the backs of the galleries to the pillars of the stage. No delicate wistfulness here: *Her* Cosima raged against the winds of fortune, raged against the Lord of Temptation, raged and railed and beat her hands against the unfairness of the world, twisted the lines that would've been hopeful in Artagne's mouth into sarcasm and cutting irony.

In the end, Saba would've willingly thrown herself at Nazeya's feet, spy or no.

The watch never showed up. The play ended to wild, screaming applause.

∼

Only two streets away from Talesyn's henge and its surrounding parkland was the Theater of Truth—a cavernous establishment in what had indeed once been an actual theater, the biggest of several in the neighborhood before the previous owners' troupe had gone bankrupt. The roof of the heavens had since been extended to cover the whole yard, which was raised to the level of the stage and floored,, and the seats of the galleries had been torn out to make room for tables and chairs.

Along the wall that had once separated stage and backstage ran the bar, perpetually sticky, backed by a vast array of kegs and bottles stacked to twice the height of a grown man. The second and third story galleries still opened into the hollow space of the center, lit by golden-burning lanterns hung at varying heights from the vaulted roof.

Enryn ordered the first round. Saba took the beer when it was brought to her and poured it down her throat. "Harder stuff," she grunted at the barkeep.

Aliss brought a bottle of menovka the size of Enryn's fist, a clear liquor from far north up the coast, rough enough to strip paint. Saba poured two fingers into her empty cup, drank it, and poured again while she waited for the wildfire burn to die out of her mouth.

"Saba," Enryn said. "You're scaring me."

She drank.

He put his hand on her wrist and moved the menovka bottle aside. "You've said four words."

"What's there to say?"

"Anything. You're Sabajan Hollant: You were born running your mouth."

She shrugged.

"Saba."

"We're done. It's over. The Reds won."

"Don't be ridiculous."

Saba slammed her cup on the table. "That play would have been Alvana's masterpiece. Our masterpiece. Pardon me if I'm being *ridiculous* about it."

A flicker in the corner of her eye—already a little foggy

from the menovka, she peered through the smoky haze, trying to spot what had snagged her attention.

Nazeya.

Saba was on her feet before she realized it, surging through the crowd. She seized Nazeya's arm and spun her around.

Nazeya caught herself on the bar, wide eyed. "Oh!" she said, then smiled. Smiled! As if she were genuinely pleased to see Saba. The little snake. "Mistress Hollant. What an unexpected pleasure."

"Unexpected," Saba said. "Is it really?"

"I'm sorry?"

"How dare you? Not a rhetorical question. Tell me true: How dare you?" Saba put her hands on the bar on either side of Nazeya and leaned in. Probably Nazeya smelled nice, but the menovka had temporarily burned out Saba's sinuses.

"How dare I...? What?"

"You know what you did."

"Did I offend you the other day?"

"How dare you," she said in a low snarl, "walk in here. And say 'Oh, Mistress Hollant!', and smile as if you and your *friends* haven't completely ruined me. How dare you?"

Nazeya's face cleared. "You were at today's performance? I realized after I walked off the other day that I didn't tell you which troupe I was in, but—well, of course you'd be able to find me—you liked the play? Er. Well. You know what I mean." She tried to nudge Saba back to get herself a little space, but Saba was immovable. "It is a very sad story, I agree. I cried four or five times in rehearsals."

"Excuse me?"

"Isn't that what you meant? The play ruined your life? Because it was so sad?"

"My life is ruined because the play was *ours*."

"Sorry?"

"Yes!" Saba snapped. "You ought to be! You ought to be far more than sorry!"

"I'm afraid I don't understand."

"You stole our play!"

"I didn't steal anything!" Nazeya drew herself up, straight and queenly, taller than Saba by seven or eight inches. "I think you've probably had too much to drink, Mistress Hollant."

Saba laughed. "Oh, you're good! I see why Yermekov sent you to spy on me."

Nazeya turned back to the bar.

Saba wedged herself in beside her and set both elbows on the counter. "Good tactic," she said. "'Dismissive' is easier than 'shocked'. More effective at disarming me, too, making me doubt myself. Smart choice."

"Mistress Hollant. I consider you one of the greatest players in the city. I'd thought that in person you must be as noble and gracious as the parts you play on stage. Silly of me, I suppose. Please leave me in peace with my grief at finding out that you're just as human as the rest of us."

"I almost believe you. Almost."

"Believe me or not. I'm not even a shareholder in the Reds. I play whatever they give me. I was lucky to get any part at all, you know. I've been auditioning for two years."

Saba scoffed. "You didn't think it was strange that Yermekov produced from thin air a play a hundred times more brilliant than anything she'd ever written before?"

Nazeya gave an elegant shrug. "I thought it was in keeping with her standard."

"Oh *please*. She's nothing compared to Alvana Stillgrail and you *know* it. You might as well admit why you were skulking around our theater the other day."

"I wasn't skulking."

"Oh? Pray tell what were you doing there, then, just when you'd conveniently happen to run into me."

"My sister lives a few streets over. I was visiting her."

Saba laughed outright. "Admit it, mes Akhal! You were there to pump me for information!"

"If you care to recall," Nazeya snapped. "I didn't press you for anything. Nor did you offer anything! We barely exchanged more than pleasantries, but apparently that's cause enough to suspect me of being a spy?"

"It is if you're a Red."

"If you think your play was stolen, then I'm sorry. If you think my troupe did it, I'm doubly sorry. It's terrible that we've all been reduced to petty squabbling. Everyone says it wasn't like this before."

Before the fashion, she meant. Before having a pet artist became the most elegant accessory for the nobility—and if one artist was good, why not a whole troupe of them? It *had* been different before.

Nazeya was still talking. "I wish I could offer to help, in the spirit of making peace, but there's nothing I can do. I'm not a shareholder. I don't get a say in anything. If I want to be paid, I take the parts Zitka Yermekov hands me."

"Even though she's a thief?"

"No one else has given me a chance." She looked despairingly at Saba. "Could I buy you a drink?"

"What," said Saba.

"I would genuinely do anything in my power to make this right, and that's the only thing there is. Stupid gesture, probably. Still. Could I?"

"Yes," said Saba's mouth—it was instinctive, accepting a drink from a pretty girl. Even if she was a Red.

Back in the good old days, the rivalry wouldn't have mattered so much. She and Nazeya could have had a spicy little fling—like the one Alvana had had with Yermekov, years ago. Eons, it seemed now. They'd even *moved in together.*

Hadn't lasted long past that, but... Well, those days were long past.

Nazeya did seem sincere, though, and if she wasn't a shareholder, then there really wasn't anything she could do, not if she wanted to keep her job. Theater troupes were not so plentiful that one could be snobbish about who one wanted to work for. One could be moral or one could be employed.

"Listen," she said, when Nazeya had ordered the drinks. "I'm... sorry. I'm a bit drunk right now."

"It's all right." It didn't sound like it was all right.

"I'm not usually like this."

"Of course. It is an extraordinary circumstance."

She was being so *polite*, despite her obvious disillusionment. Fuck. Saba could've kicked herself. Nazeya had admired her work, allegedly (*genuinely*, Saba's vanity insisted, and perhaps her drink-muddled reason was coming to agree). Saba had ruined that for her forever.

They sat in silence until the drinks arrived—Nazeya had a cup of beer; Saba, another thimble of menovka. She slammed it back in one go. It burned all the way down. She would have wheezed for breath if she hadn't been standing next to a pretty girl. *Posturing* for the pretty girl, as if—well.

"You were good," Saba said thickly. "In the play. You didn't act it like I would've, but—Yermekov's a shitty director. The things wrong with it were her fault. You did it all by yourself, didn't you?"

Nazeya shrugged. "Yes, mostly. She tells us where to stand, that's about it. She gives us free rein on our own performances."

"You should make more eye contact with the others. More connection. Like you're reaching out to them, but with your voice. And—sorry, do you want me to tell you this?" A beat, and then Saba snorted. "But why would you? I'm just some angry drunk lady."

"We don't have much else to talk about." Nazeya swirled her beer in her cup slowly, looking down into it as she said softly, "A few days ago I would've tripped at the chance to hear Sabajan Hollant tell me what she thought of my performance."

She wasn't tripping now, Saba noted, and kicked herself again. "Cosima should be sadder. Sad and quiet to wrench at the heart." Nazeya said nothing. Saba forged onwards. "You play her as *angry*. You ought to play her as lonely. Desperately lonely and trying to hide it, trying to give enough of herself away that maybe other people will give something back and she won't be so empty."

Nazeya said softly, "I hadn't thought of her like that."

"She's a good liar, Cosima is. Play her with a little secret sadness, a little desperation, and you'll have the yard flooded an inch deep in tears. I swear it."

"I may well try that. Thank you." She sipped her drink. "Who would you have played, if—if."

"The Lord of Temptation," Saba said, feeling a smile curl at the corner of her mouth.

"You would have been... something. Really something."

"That part was made for me," Saba said, and was pleased to see Nazeya nod immediately. She felt most kinship with Talesyn, of course, but Idunet was a close second. "Yermekov's doing it all wrong. She doesn't move like she's got any cock at all, and the Lord of Temptation—he ought to swagger. She plays him..." Saba frowned, thinking. "She plays him like how *she* seduces. She's an ice queen. She wants to sit on her throne and have people fall at her feet in supplication without lifting a finger."

"Not inaccurate," Nazeya murmured into her cup.

"Right? So the Lord of Temptation should be—" Saba gestured grandly. "A man walking out of a brothel with both his purses lighter. Or a queen striding into the throne room of a country she's just conquered. The Lord of Temptation is active, not passive. He's the seducer of the world! He should *seduce*, not wait for his victims to fall at his feet in awe. Like— here, Yermekov does this, watch." Saba drew herself up into an approximation of Yermekov's posture: stiff and regal, chin raised, expression cold and smug. 'I, who whisper into kings' ears," she intoned, 'until their fingers twitch with greed and strain to raise their weapons or their wits to conquer what those twitching fingers seize."

Nazeya bit her lip to suppress a smile. 'Very like her."

Saba's vanity purred. Idunet, that rat bastard, kept her damn mouth kept talking: 'See, but here's how I'd do it." She leaned in close to Nazeya, letting her eyes go hooded and hot, and licked her lips. 'I, who turns a maiden's eye and *plucks* her purse until both weep," she breathed, her voice full of promise.

'No, lord," Nazeya said. She sounded a little breathless. 'I have an altogether different quest. In supplication do I call to you."

'Ahhhh." Saba smiled long and slow. She traced one finger along the inside of Nazeya's wrist and was pleased to see goose-bumps bloom in her wake. 'A supplication. Now I see. The whelp aspires to a libertine? How many battles hast thou fought, young whelp? I do not waste my gifts on untried swords. And tell me true, how many maiden's purses hast thou clutched?" Teasing, then, beckoning, a suggestion of laughter: 'A supplication must demand some coin."

'I've fought no battles, Lord, in love or war," Nazeya said. The light had come back to her eyes, Saba was pleased to see. She made no move to pull her wrist away from Saba's touch. 'Nor touched a purse that was not freely offered me."

'A little monk thou art, then, not a libertine at all. Dost take thy ecstasy in virtue, then?"

'Oh Lord, I beg you, hear my words. Temptation's Lord

you are, the lord of sin and pleasure both—I beg for pleasure, Lord, in truth, a pleasure such the world has rarely seen."

"Beg for pleasure, dost thou, lad?" Saba purred. She traced her touch up Nazeya's arm to her shoulder, her neck. Maybe Lord Talesyn and his baby brother were quarreling and that's why Dream-plucker was fucking with her—it was the only explanation, because she was absolutely *nailing* this. "Now speakst my mother tongue, young whelp. Pray tell, what rare and wondrous pleasure dost thou seek?"

"True love."

"True love!" Saba barked a laugh and dropped her hand. She took Nazeya's cup instead and sipped from it, smiling over the rim. "In faith, a pleasure far too rare for even I, a humble merchant of the fleshly joys, to make my trade."

"The mistress of my heart is far from me, though separated are we only by a city's span, if that," Nazeya entreated. "My mistress longs for me, and I for her, and if we were but brought together—"

"Peace! I care not for thy heartstruck witterings, young whelp: A merchant am I, not a priest to hear your sorrows and your woes." Saba snorted, then looked Nazeya over thoughtfully. "If truly speakst thou, why, I'll name my price, and sell thee pleasure such as none have known."

"Then name it, Lord, I'll pay in every coin I have and more."

"Anon, anon, I'll do so in good time." Saba said with a dismissive wave. "Thou'lt pay my price when all is said and done. Our contract is a promise, we two men of honor will abide. Like merchants, then, we clasp our hands together, palm to palm, to call the contract made," Saba extended her hand for Nazeya to shake, "and unlike merchants, heartstruck whelp, thou signst thy name upon it with a kiss."

She hadn't looked away from Nazeya's eyes even once. They were so close, she was a hand-span away from her... and then the Lord of Temptation's confidence vanished like morning mist.

Saba took her hand back, cleared her throat, turned away. She hadn't felt her heart fluttering like this for years. Decades, maybe. *Idunet, the things I do for you!* she thought plaintively. *The things I do, Seductor of the World! But you never go easy on me, do you! Idunet, why!*

"So you can play Aucien and Cosima both," she said, trying to sound casual.

"Yes," said Nazeya. "I was hoping to play him."

"You should. Dauren's shit compared to you." That wasn't what she'd meant to say. Fuck. "Listen, I'm drunk. I'm sorry for shouting at you before, and I'm sorry for... for showing off."

"It's nothing," Nazeya said quickly. "Reciting with you is an honor I never dreamed of."

"Ahaha," said Saba. "Haha. Yes. Well. This is probably wildly unwelcome, but if you'd ever like to audition for the Lights... Just walk in. Day or night. Middle of a performance, I don't care. I'll hear you. And if you needed any incentive, *we* aren't thieves."

"That's very kind of you, but I'm under contract."

Saba frowned at her. "You're what?"

"It's something Yermekov came up with."

"Like with writers?" Saba had a couple contracts with playwrights in the city—three princes for a new play, half paid upfront upon agreement, half on delivery of the finished pages.

"More like with soldiers."

"Talesyn's teeth! Is she exploiting you?"

"No! Not at all. The terms were... more than fair."

"Soldiers sign up for a year, or five years, or ten years. Is that...?"

"Yes."

"And how long do you have left?"

"Two years and three months."

"Shit." Saba put her elbows on the bar and dropped her head into her hands. She should've sworn by Mategat, the Lady of Time, not Talesyn. Two *years*. "*Shit*."

"I believe," Nazeya said with a nervous little laugh, "that it's to prevent things like this from happening."

"I'm not trying to *poach* you."

"You just offered me an audition at any hour of the day or night."

Saba groaned. "How'd the contract even happen?"

"They told me that's how they did things. They said that it protected me as much as it protected them—they can't just turn me out on the street, and it says how much I get paid for each play, and when the money's due, and so on. It sounded like a good idea at the time."

"At the time."

"Still," Nazeya corrected. "It *still* seems like a good idea. I don't blame them at all. Loyalty is worth a lot."

"Well, you should probably tell them that you spoke to me, then. If you're so loyal." Saba drained her cup. "Congratulations on your play," she said, and stalked back to Enryn.

Nearly an hour later, when she was almost literally blind with drunkenness, one of the barmaids slipped her a bit of paper.

I'm not going to tell them. I won't tell anyone; we need not even mention that we met, it read. *And let this prove that my apology was sincere. I didn't know, truly.*

"All I asked of you," the Lord Chancellor said in a low, vicious voice when he met Saba just outside the courthouse, "was to have a new Stillgrail play for me this season. This petty squabbling is *unbecoming* of the troupe carrying my name."

He was dressed in plain clothes—somber greens and dull browns without trim or decoration. Incognito, as much as a man of his social stature could be.

"Yes, my lord." Adding his name to the troupe had granted them nothing but bragging rights and the occasional invitation to perform at elegant functions. Even the money wasn't much better than it had been before.

"If you had not made such a mess of this," he said slowly, as if he were explaining something to a child, "I would have asked if you were sure."

Saba stifled the instinctive swell of anger.

"And then," he continued, "I would have gone to the Lord Seneschal. I would have looped him into another round of our dance, the little game that we have been playing against each other for three decades now. I would have threatened him with a smile and called it check, if not checkmate. He would have gone to his troupe and told them to delay. He would have told them to perform something else. And all of this would be handled discreetly. *Privately*. In little rooms by little clerks, do you see?"

"Yes, my lord," she said.

"How will it be handled now?" He gestured to the court-house looming before them. "Public spectacle."

"Alvana has proof," Saba said quietly. "She has papers."

"You'd better hope that she does. You're becoming an embarrassment to me, Hollant."

❧

The Lord Chancellor's Players brought their suit against the Lord Seneschal's Women for fraud, theft, and several other complaints that Saba didn't bother committing to memory.

The Lord Seneschal's Women professed themselves shocked at such allegations and submitted for the justice's perusal three stacks of documents, each as high as Saba's knee, proving their ownership of the play *Some by Virtue Fall.*

There were copies of the script written in Zitka Yermekov and Verity Dauren's own hands, which they demonstrated before the court for further proof. There were no fewer than five separate drafts of the play with swathes of lines scribbled out and scrawls of marginalia. There was a full complement of correspondence between Yermekov and Dauren, most of which seemed to be discussing either their plans for staging the play, ideas one of them had had in the middle of the night, or suggestions meet up and work on it in person.

With shaking hands, Alvana presented her five clean copies of the script as counter-evidence.

If Saba hadn't spent months watching her write the play, if she hadn't seen Alvana in the mornings with stained fingers and fine splatters of ink on her cuffs and an unslept glassiness to her eyes, if she hadn't listened to Alvana muttering lines until each phrase was a perfect jewel, if she hadn't on countless occasions answered Alvana's requests for a word that would rhyme with her previous line... If she hadn't watched Alvana slowly crumple up her current page and toss it into the fire and start anew...

If Saba hadn't been able to swear beyond a shadow of a doubt that Alvana Stillgrail was the true author of *Some by Virtue Fall*, she too might well have looked at the mountain of paper provided by the Lord Seneschal's Women and seen what the judge saw.

"It seems to me that the evidence is overwhelming," said the judge. "I hereby dismiss the suit brought by the Lord Chancellor's Players as unfounded. May the Lord of Law and Lady of Truth bless my words and deem the verdict fair."

Saba stormed out of the courtroom with the bang of the

gavel still ringing in her ears, shouldering through the chattering crowd until she burst out through the doors. She stood there on the courthouse steps, shaking, every muscle in her body tight with fury. Alvana followed just after her, weeping into her handkerchief.

"I'm sorry," Alvana choked out. "I burned the drafts and the notes. I thought it was safer. I thought they'd steal *those*."

"It isn't your fault," Saba gritted out.

"N-next time, we'll—we'll get a proper lawyer and I'll give her copies of everything, and—"

"Miss Stillgrail," said the Lord Chancellor. Saba flinched. She didn't even have to turn around to feel him bearing down upon them. Out of the corner of her eye, she saw him take Alvana by the arm. "Miss Stillgrail, perhaps you can explain to me *what just happened in there*."

"I don't know," Alvana said, gulping down her tears. "I thought they were going to try to steal my drafts, but they— I'm sorry, your lordship."

"Oh, what a relief," he said. Saba glanced at his hand on Alvana's elbow—his knuckles were white, Alvana's plump arm deeply dimpled by the harshness of his grip. "What a relief, that you're *sorry*."

"Your lordship," Saba said softly. "You're hurting her."

"Stay out of it, Hollant," he snapped, without taking his eyes from Alvana. "I deigned to patronize your ragamuffin little troupe because of *you*, Miss Stillgrail. Players," and this word he spat like it was bitter, overbrewed tea, "can be scraped off the street for pennies. But they can't do anything without a play, can they?"

"No, your lordship," Alvana whispered. A lie, of course—they'd improvised whole performances before, mostly when they were younger, drunker, stupider.

Alvana tried to tug her arm away, but the Lord Chancellor tightened his grip until she squeaked. "The conditions of my patronage," he continued, voice shifting to silk and honey-cakes, "Included that I would see three new Alvana Stillgrail plays a year. And now not only do you *lose* one of them, but you were incompetent enough to—"

"Your lordship," Saba said again, just barely daring to touch her fingertips to his hand where it was bruising Alvana's arm. "Miss Stillgrail works hard. There is no need to fear. As long as we guard against further sabotage, you'll have your plays."

At last, he released her, flicking his eyes once more back to Saba. "My patience grows very thin indeed."

"Yes, your lordship. We appreciate your generosity in these difficult times." *Fuck you,* she thought at him as hard as she could, dropping her eyes so he couldn't see the words written across them in letters of fire. *Nobody touches Alvana like that. A word from her and I'd murder you right here on the steps of the courthouse, and to hell with the consequences.* "There won't be any more incidents, unless the Lord Seneschal's Women start something themselves. I'll be sure to keep you better apprised of the situation. No more incidents."

"See that there aren't," he said coldly, and stalked away.

Saba touched Alvana's arm as soon as he was out of earshot. "Are you all right?"

"Yes." She'd stopped crying, at least. That was something. "It fucking hurts, though."

"You'll have a wicked bruise. Like a peach, you are." Alvana only nodded, rubbing her elbow. Saba's eyes stung; she dug her fingernails into her palms and refused, *refused* to let the sting develop into tears. "*Do* you have anything else written? Anything close to finished?".

"Not much. Some poems, some fragments."

"Shit."

"Yes, that's a good word to describe it. Worst stuff I've ever written." She sniffled. "What if we just... gave up? What's the point? We might as well go to the countryside and—and raise pigs."

"Of *course* we're not giving up." Saba longed for a carafe of coffee to shatter against a wall. "Used to be that something like this would happen and the boys would go off to punch their feelings and—and for five minutes I'd *understand*. I'd cheer for them as they went. Hell, I went with them sometimes, but..."

"Skinny," Alvana said, voice going thick with tears once more. "Snap like a twig."

"Yeah."

"You hate pain."

"*Yeah*," Saba said vehemently. "Later on, I wouldn't be so understanding. I'd just be annoyed that we were stuck in a gods-damned children's feud instead of letting each other be. But right now," she growled, "I understand again."

Alvana's breath hitched. "Saba, what are we going to *do*?"

She'd been asking Saba that for twenty-five years now. Every time, Saba remembered the first time, remembered two little girls—one dark-skinned and serious and scrawny, one very chubby and rosy-pink all over, with rosy-pink ribbons in her hair and on her dress—both nine years old, both friendless and lonely and feeling like they didn't quite fit into the world, both trying valiantly to play together as if the loneliness wasn't eating them both up, both just a little too careless in their efforts—remembered them looking together in horror at the jagged shards scattered on the ground at their feet like so many jewels, at the hole they'd smashed in a fine stained glass window in the temple shrine on the estate where the little pink girl's father lived. Looking at each other. Silently vowing to be friends forever if they could get out of this mess. And the little pink girl, breath hitching with tears as she said, for the first time out of thousands, "Saba, what are we going to do?"

Just as she had then, Saba took a breath and nodded grimly at the problem. "We're going to keep the doors open.

We're going to go to your father's house and ransack his library for plays that are old enough to be new again. That'll buy you time to finish something."

~

Saba stood in the theater yard and surveyed her troops over the edge of her coffee cup. Several books borrowed from Tulio Stillgrail's library were stacked on the table beside her. A few copies of one of Alvana's really ancient plays, *A Midwinter's Ball,* had been distributed to the troupe. It would do, no matter how much Alvana sighed that the play wasn't even worth the paper it was written on. It was not what Saba would have considered Alvana's greatest work—it had been popular enough ten years ago when it was new, but it had faded quickly in the public's memory into nothing more than a recollection of mirth.

They had to put on *some* play. The ones in their current circulation were going to start getting old sooner than anyone liked to think about. A different play every day—except Ystraday, because Saba had always felt that was her bad-luck day— six plays per week, about twenty-four every month... They *had* to get fresh material.

Nothing to do but fling themselves off the cliff and hope the wind caught them.

"All right," Saba said, "let's try this again."

The casting was uninspired—Artagne was Melisande again and seemed lukewarm about reprising the role. Saba had endeavored to mix up the others and scatter them through the ensemble, but it seemed... strained. There was no fire to it, no tension, no excitement.

Even amongst the newcomers, there was only a vague shimmer of interest. It made Saba's teeth itch. It wasn't their job to be thrilled with her decisions—their job was to shut up until she told them to speak their lines, and then to *declaim* them from the sawdust to the rafters and turn her blood to sparkling wine.

Iracena was running her mouth again, Talesyn have fucking mercy. "I don't see why we're not still doing the old play."

"This is the old play," Saba grunted.

"The old new play. *Some by Virtue Fall*."

Saba prayed for patience. "Iracena, darling, did you somehow miss the heartbreaking and messy trial we just endured last week? Because if you'd just told me you had your head stuck too far up your own ass to pay attention to anything going on around you, we could have arranged the proper accommodations for your condition."

"It's ours, isn't it?" Iracena said, *just* this side of snapping. "Why don't we just put it on?"

"Not ours according to the rule of law, chickadee. *Some by Virtue Fall* will go down in history as Yermekov and Dauren's greatest work and unusually masterful for them." She set her coffee aside. "Let's run through the opening dance. Pair up however. We'll fret about actual couples later." Saba vaulted onto the stage and snatched up Artagne's hand herself; Artagne gave her a faux-indulgent smile and a sincere squeeze of her hand. "Right, everyone ready?"

It was a miracle they didn't all fall off the stage.

"Well," said Saba when the scrimmage had concluded a few minutes later. "That was a shipwreck, wasn't it."

"None of us dance the men's parts very often, that's the problem," said Alvana as she untangled herself from the heap of Iracena, Lutha, and Ishmeta and struggled back to her feet.

"I beg your pardon, I dance the men's parts all the time," Saba said.

"That's because you like girls who only know how to dance the woman's part."

"Exactly."

Alvana sighed. "Let's try it again—women turn *left*, men turn *right*. Or, you know, whoever is playing men. Saba, get off the stage. You're not even in this scene."

"Am I permitted no small joys in life? I want to dance with Artagne."

"I daresay you can dance with Artagne any night at the Theater of Truth if you ask her very gallantly," Alvana said. "Go boss us around from over there where you can see what's going on."

Saba grumbled and dropped off the stage. She sat on top of her table in the yard and watched them muddle through the opening dance several more times, occasionally yelling instructions at them and then clambering back up onto the boards to shove them around until they did as she wanted. Between runs, she flicked through the books from Alvana's father's library. Old dusty things, most of them, almost all of them hand-scribed. A few were in languages besides Avaren, and Saba set these aside for special scrutiny. A foreign play would likely be unfamiliar to their audiences—unfamiliar, and therefore *new*.

In the next scene, she watched Artagne-as-Melisande sashay back and forth across the stage, fluttering a fan below her face as she drawled her lines and smoldered across the boards at Iracena, who had been really the only option for the lead role, Roderigo, Melisande's sworn enemy and, by the end of the play, her true love. Saba had to give her credit—no one else in the cast did stuffy, vain nobility like Iracena did. Her accent? Improving, but still painful. Her *demeanor*, though? Simply splendid.

The main problem was that Saba was bored out of her mind every time she had to watch them kiss.

"Talesyn's *tits*," she shrieked at them after their third comprehensive failure to depict convincing passion.

"Artagne, darling, you're fine, besides the fact that it looks like you're kissing *a wooden log*. Iracena! What the fuck is going on up there? I'd swear in court that you'd never been kissed before."

"I haven't," she snapped, red-faced.

Saba gave her a withering look. "Well, now you have, and lucky you: Your first kiss was the gorgeous and unparalleled Artagne Grey. Tell that to your grandchildren in forty or fifty years! Now, get over yourself and show me that you've got some fire in your crotch!"

"Can't you tell me what you want me to *do*?"

Saba leapt onto the boards. She charged up to Iracena, seized her face in both hands, pulled her close—and *paused*.

She burned her gaze into Iracena's.

She breathed.

She parted her lips.

She kissed Iracena like she was starved for it, pushing forward until Iracena had to lean back, catching Saba's shoulders for balance.

"That's how," Saba said, breaking away. "And now you can tell your grandchildren that your second kiss was the magnificent and unrivaled Sabajan Hollant."

"Not unrivaled," Iracena said, wiping her mouth with the back of her hand. She grinned like shards of glass. "Zitka Yermekov exists."

Saba froze. She felt, distantly, Artagne lay a hand on her arm and murmur her name.

"No time for this," Talsyn said. "We have a play this afternoon."

"I'd throw you out of the troupe today if I could," Saba said in a low voice, her eyes not leaving Iracena's.

"You need me," she replied. "Stop speaking to me like I'm your scullery maid."

"I'll speak to you however I please."

"No *time* for this," Talsyn said again, louder. "We have to finish this and refresh on Haught's play before lunch."

Artagne tugged at Saba's arm. "Let it go." Saba let herself be tugged, easing away from Iracena but holding her glare until Artagne herded her to the steps down into the yard. "She's a puppy," Artagne murmured. "She's nipping at you to get your attention. It's not worth the fight."

Saba had never met any slight rudeness that wasn't worth the fight.

～

That afternoon's performance was a bright comedy they'd bought a few weeks before the Edict from Wisym Haught—not the best of the writers in the city, not by a long shot, and Saba hadn't even had to work to memorize his play. Its jokes were so tired and its beats were so mathematical in their timing that one read had been enough to affix the general gist of it in her mind. Utter rubbish, but Haught had been in a bit of a financial bind, and she'd already paid him an advance on another play. For the sake of seeing that one finished, she'd agreed to take this one off his hands in exchange for paying his bar tab and keeping him out of debtor's prison—but she'd gotten the short end of the stick *twice,* somehow. Hadn't Haught mentioned something about how grateful he was, because no one else seemed to care at all about his work?

There were some few benefits here—not in the text itself, of course, but staging and interpretation could fix a world of sins. Saba pranced thither and yon across the stage in her boyish faun costume and draped herself across Artagne's bosom at every opportunity, which was probably the main benefit to be found in this play.

The audience, only half-filling the theater, gave an appreciative chuckle; Saba nuzzled her nose further into Artagne's cleavage and recited some joke of Haught's without bothering to pay attention to it. Another weak laugh rippled through the crowd. Artagne, playing at outrage, flung her off. They traded lines that should have been bitingly funny and which managed only a gentle gnaw. Not even a gnaw—they *gummed*.

The faun, frightened off, hid behind one of the pillars. Artagne-as-whatshername made a raunchy speech to reveal her motivations and whirled offstage. A moment later, Saba peeked out from the pillar, looked around, and gave the audience an enormous wink.

In Haught's text, the faun's monologue was far, far too long. Nearly thirty lines, which Saba would have gloried in if it had been written by any half-competent playwright. Haught was an infuriating mediocrity, and Saba was exhausted at the very thought of having to declaim her way through phrases that were just awkward enough to fit strangely in her mouth but not so much that the laypeople would particularly notice.

Oh, screw this, she thought, only five or six lines into it. She improvised the rest on the fly, revealing the faun's plan for erotic mischief in half the space, and even fit in a few amusing puns on familiar lines from other, better playwrights. When she danced bowlegged offstage, as if burdened by an unrelenting erection, the audience's laughter was significantly more substantial, followed by somewhat more than a smattering of applause.

Saba ducked backstage, heard Talsyn's footsteps as he smoothly took her place and began to recite. She couldn't bring herself to listen.

"Saba," Artagne hissed, catching her arm. "Are you all right?"

"Bored to death, my beauty, my goddess," Saba answered. "How are you?"

"I've been better. It's not a great play."

"It's not even a good play."

'But the punters like it well enough, so let's be a little respectful, eh?" Artagne pinched her arm. 'We don't need any more antics from you."

'I only committed antics when I was alone! I wouldn't throw you anything like that without warning."

'Mm," Artagne said. 'Not just that. You held back out there."

Saba boggled at her. 'Beg pardon?"

'Oh, hell, Saba, you flirt with me all the time if there's no audience, but on stage you're a perfect *gentleman*."

'You take that *back*, madam. Shall I demand satisfaction?"

'It's a lewd play," Artagne said. 'It's supposed to be a lewd play. Stop trying to elevate it and give me something to work with. If you don't at least grab my ass in the next scene, I'm going to be offended."

'No one has suffered as I have suffered," Saba sighed.

At their cue, Saba chased Artagne onto the stage, capering and cackling—they whirled around one of the pillars until Saba caught her around the waist and dove in for a kiss; Artagne deftly dodged, sending Saba stumbling past her. It was a variety of low comedy which Saba had never been particularly fond of. She burbled through the lines, declaring the faun's love. She grabbed Artagne's ass as mandated, nuzzled her entire face shamelessly into Artagne's breasts, attempted to scramble beneath Artagne's skirts—which, admittedly, did get a rousing laugh from the audience. Artagne answered her effortlessly, thwarting her and rebuffing her at every turn, until at last the faun threw himself bodily to the floor and declared defeat, begging for his lady to command him as she would.

And there, flat on her back, looking up into Artagne's face, Saba caught a glimpse of... Nazeya. Nazeya, right there in the threepenny seats in the second-floor gallery, leaning on the railing and looking down with a faint smile. A goddess. For a moment, all the lines went out of Saba's head—panicked, she scrambled to find herself. Artagne was just finishing up her line; the hesitation would have been unnoticeable. Saba got through the rest of the scene in a daze and could only hope it made her faun seem lovestruck and thoroughly beguiled.

"I ask you again," Artagne said when they were safely backstage. "Are you all right? You had an odd moment out there."

"Saw someone I know." Saba cleared her throat. *A Red*, she nearly said. But no, she wouldn't speak of them now, not in the middle of the play. "Tell you later."

After that interminable production of trivial smut, they took their bows. The applause was not deafening. It was merely respectable, which was still more than this awful tripe deserved. Saba doffed her jaunty little hat and stepped forward to bow again. "Good people," she cried. "We are honored have held your attention for these short hours! Go in peace and return tomorrow for another play, a gentle romance: *My Lord's Lady-Love*, by the esteemed Angrun Blackhand! You'll laugh, you'll cry, you'll be transported!"

More applause. Blackhand was a reliable choice—a good writer, but again not what anyone could call a great one.

"We need new material," Saba muttered as she went offstage. "What are the Genehofens up to these days, do they have anything new?"

"We don't have much money to pay them with, even if they did," Alvana said.

"Poppycock, the crowds have been respectable. We must have turned a little profit today."

"Mmm, a very small one, after we pay everyone. Not enough to buy a new play."

"And you? You have anything yet?"

Alvana grunted, sighed. "No. Maybe. I don't know."

"Hurry it up, would you?" Saba grinned and clapped her on the shoulder, then turned into the dressing room. Artagne handed her a damp cloth, already busily scrubbing off her own paint. "Bless you. Was that too much?"

"On stage? No, dear, that was perfect."

"The thing with your skirt?"

"Nearly pissed myself trying not to giggle."

"While I was under there? The groundlings would've laughed to knock the house down." Saba roughly scrubbed the faun-dapple paint off her face with the cloth. "We need new material."

"Oh, right." Artagne tapped the stack of Tulio Stillgrail's books on the dresser. "I don't speak any of these languages, but I think one of them is in Mangarha."

"Damn." Saba flung the wet cloth into the bucket, pulled on her proper clothes, dried off her hands, tucked the books under her arm. "Thanks anyway, gorgeous."

Mabeth popped her head through the door. "Saba, there's a visitor for you."

"Eh? Who?" She turned, and—

Nazeya.

"Why are you in my backstage?" Saba demanded. "Who let you in here? What have you seen? Get out." She lunged and seized Nazeya's arm, dragging her through the back of the theater towards the alley entrance.

"Ow," Nazeya said politely.

"Why are you here?" Saba hissed.

"To extend an olive branch. To say sorry again. I heard about the trial."

They reached the vestibule where all the troupe's coats were hung. Saba stopped and put her hands on her hips. "Really. That's it?"

"I wanted to see you perform. I wanted to support your troupe."

"Nazeya, you—" Saba pinched the bridge of her nose. "You can't do this. How would it go if I showed up at yours again? You might not care, but Yermekov and Dauren would. Do they know you're here?"

"Of course not. It's my day off. They can't tell me what to do with my free time."

"You sure? How closely did you read the terms of that contract?"

"Extremely."

Saba dug through the rack until she found her coat, a battered old thing in the Vintish style, which always made Artagne misty-eyed when Saba wore it—green wool with large cuffs and bright brass buttons she kept polished to a high shine. "The others can't know that you're a Red, so just—go. Please. Leave. Sorry. Here, I've got a few pennies, I'll refund your seat—" She patted down her coat, one handed, the books still clamped under her elbow.

"Please don't. I'm not here for anything—I just wanted to say sorry again, and that I liked the performance today. And reciting with you at the Truth. I like all your performances—as a professional colleague, I mean—"

Saba found a few coins in the bottom of a pocket. She counted out three pennies, the price for the second story gallery where Nazeya had sat, and held them out. "Here. Here you are." Nazeya put her hands behind her back, shaking her head. Saba huffed. "Look, I'm sorry too, but I have to protect my family first. Please just go." She pushed the coins at Nazeya; Nazeya pushed her hand away, and Saba lost her grip on the books, which tumbled to the floor. "Fuck!"

"Sorry—sorry—"

They both knelt. "These aren't mine," Saba grumbled. "They'd better not be damaged—"

One of them, the Mangarha book, had fallen open to the title page. Nazeya's hand paused on it before she picked it up.

"You can't do this again, do you understand?" Saba said

gently. "I'm really sorry about it, but you can't. You get it, don't you?" She held her hand out for the book.

"Why do you have this?" Nazeya asked quietly, gazing down at the book's title page.

Saba stopped breathing. She didn't know what that book was, other than something from Papa Stillgrail's library, and therefore probably rare and valuable, or at the very least eccentric.

And Nazeya could be a spy. There was no proof either way.

Saba snatched the book away and stood up. "It's nothing."

Nazeya's expression was unreadable; she rose more slowly.

"So I have something in Mangarha," Saba said with a nervous laugh. "What of it? Lots of people speak Mangarha. Especially in Mangar-Khagra. It could be anything. A gift from my Khagri granny."

"Is it a gift from your Khagri granny?"

"It's private, is what it is," Saba said. She turned Nazeya bodily and pushed her out the door. "No point in coming back, you know. If the girls find out that you're a Red, they won't let you inside. Anyway, I'm off to the bar, bye!" She scuttled off down the street—or attempted to.

"Saba," Nazeya caught up in two strides and kept pace with her. "Do you know how to speak Mangarha?"

"Nope, not a word! Goodbye!"

"Do you want to read that book? My grandmother *is* Mangarhan—I could translate it for you. As an apology."

Fuck. No one in the troupe had even been able to identify the language it was written in. The time and legwork it would take to track down another translator—not to mention the money to pay them—wasn't in great supply these days.

On the other hand: Trusting a Red? Handing it over?

"I could at least tell you what book it is," Nazeya said desperately.

Saba groaned and ducked into an alleyway—nobody needed to see her fraternizing with the enemy. "Fine," she said, pulling it from the stack. Then they'd *both* know whether it was worth the trouble for the Reds to steal it from her.

Nazeya took another long look at the title, her beautiful lips moving slowly. Saba tried not to stare at them.

A great rush of breath went out of Nazeya. "It says *Two Moons and Twelve Stars*," she said, her voice a little shaky. "I—I was surprised before, I thought I must've misread it..."

Saba crossed her arms. "You've heard of it?"

"I... Yes. Can I ask, sorry, where'd you get this?"

Saba snatched it away from her again. "None of your business, gorgeous, sorry."

"Please, I'm just curious."

"Bet you are. I'll ask someone else." Saba shoved it in her pocket and charged out of the alley. The bar, yes. A whole cask of ale would do to drown the memory of the day's performance and, as a bonus, that of this painfully lovely woman pleading with her.

Nazeya appeared at her elbow again. "It's a famous book," Nazeya said urgently, "by Suri Erhabar, one of the greatest Mangarha poets who ever lived."

"Poetry? Lovely." That'd save her some time. If the book had any longer narrative poems, perhaps Alvana could adapt one into something performable.

"Poetry and essays. And commentary, but—please, just tell me where you found that copy."

"Tell me why it matters so much."

"It's a famous Mangarhan book—it's a *part of me*. Saba, please. I've never seen a copy in real life, and my family are booksellers."

Saba didn't answer, but Nazeya dogged her steps all the way through the warren of streets and across the wide green sward of Talhenge—the holy circle of ancient standing stones dedicated to Lord Talesyn—then back into the warren of streets on the other side, all the way to the Theater of Truth, all the way to the bar, and thence into the darkest corner with Saba and her drink.

Nazeya sat beside her, expression beseeching; Saba felt herself wavering and mentally groaned a curse at Dreamplucker and his little whispers of temptation.

"I can't trust you." She had to force the words out.

Nazeya sat down beside her and took her hand; Saba's heart and stomach swooped. "For this, you can. I swear it." Saba took a long draft of her beer and ignored how her fingers curled around Nazeya's. She couldn't help it; they had a mind of their own. "If there's anything I could do to prove that I'm not trying to cheat you..."

Saba stroked the back of Nazeya's soft brown hand with her thumb. "How long have you been a player?"

"A few years, just bit parts. I only contracted with the Reds a couple months before the Edict."

Saba drew her hand away with a wrenching reluctance. "Then you'd remember how it used to be. Back when all the troupes were independent, back before we owed fealty to anyone."

"Only a little. It was already changing by the time I got started."

"It wasn't always this... this *vicious*. Before, it was just posturing, peacocking, pranks. Maybe the occasional bar-fight. But when we got patrons, the stakes seemed... higher. So the boys went and started a war. You can bet the rest of us will be *finishing* it."

"Yes," Nazeya whispered.

"Only a matter of time until theft becomes murder." The beer was already beginning to reach Saba's head. "Make a start on proving your trustworthiness and answer me this: Is it as bad for you lot as it is for us? Having these lordly patrons?"

'It's... not as good as it was before. We can't perform whatever we like."

'What do you expect? Making money's what they care about most."

'Plays don't make money," Nazeya said with a humorless laugh. 'If plays made money, everyone would want to join the theater."

'Mm. But those fine lords care about reputation, too. *Politics*."

Nazeya nodded, silent for a moment before she said, 'Ours gave us a list of all the plays we're not allowed to perform, all the playwrights we're not allowed to buy from. Broader restrictions, too. Like forbidding satire."

Saba snorted. 'That explains why the Reds have been leaning so hard on the serious and dour shit. I thought maybe Yermekov's monthly visitor had overstayed its welcome."

Nazeya shook her head. 'The Lord Seneschal is extremely wary of anything with a humorous bent to it. He's terrified of being laughed at. He thinks everything we do is a deliberate attempt to humiliate him."

Saba threw her hands in the air. 'Talesyn's fucking teeth! Why does he keep your troupe in patronage, then?"

'Because if he didn't, then *your* patron would have something that *ours* doesn't, and that really would be humiliating."

'It's not worth it. We don't get much more money this way. We aren't protected from debt. We still have to pay for almost everything ourselves." Seething, Saba finished her beer.

'If we didn't have patrons," Nazeya said softly, 'then we wouldn't be fighting like we are. And maybe then you wouldn't think I was a spy—"

'Oh, I'd probably still think you were a spy, but a different kind. More mischiefy, more sexy. Well. Not more sexy, pretty much the same sexy as now." *Still, tongue, still!* Saba rebuked herself.

"And maybe," Nazeya continued, a blush in her voice if not on her cheeks, "then you'd show me the Erhabar book."

Saba huffed. "Fixated on it, are you?"

"It's important to me. Please. Saba, I *swear*—"

"Bah!" Saba stood abruptly from the table. "I'll *think* about it. I'll *think!*"

By all the gods, you could light palaces with Nazeya's eyes when they shone like that. Saba tore herself away and staggered downstairs, drunk more on woman than she was on wine. Or beer, rather, but that didn't alliterate.

Perhaps... perhaps. Surely it wouldn't harm anything to let Nazeya look at it, would it? And if she were to translate it, wouldn't that be a lovely present for Alvana, even if there wasn't anything useful for the troupe? It'd cheer her up, at least—gods knew she needed cheering, after the year they'd been having.

Saba stomped to the bar and had just called for a refill when a flash of chestnut hair in the corner of her eye caught her attention. She turned and glared straight at Iracena. What was *she* doing here? Hadn't she bothered to stay behind and help tidy up the theater? All the newcomers had to, and the shareholders drew lots before the plays. Saba's luck was usually excellent, but if it hadn't been, she'd be collecting trash and raking the sawdust with the rest of them.

She stalked to Iracena's table and dropped heavily into a chair. "You all finish up early?"

"The cleaning, you mean? I finished my part, yes."

"Your part?"

"Artagne told me to collect all the cushions from the galleries and put them away. I finished that, so I left."

Saba bit her tongue. No, a retort or a rebuke would not do. Iracena was new, and she was allowed one stupid moment. "Next time, you should ask the shareholders what other chores they want you to do. Not polite to just leave."

"You *ought* to hire someone for all those nasty jobs."

Saba didn't like her tone. "I don't like your tone."

"Am I *wrong*? The Reds don't sweep filth and trash."

"Good for them! We decided it's more economical if everyone *pulls their own weight*."

Iracena drew herself up, queenly and outraged. Saba noted little aspects of her posture and movement for use on stage later. "I don't like *your* tone."

"You don't have to endure it. You can go join another troupe. Or you can go back and *help the others*." Saba stared her down. Did the young chit think she could push Sabajan Hollant around? No one else did. "Make a choice. You're part of the troupe, or you're not. Choose."

"What about you?"

"What about me?"

"What would the others say if they knew you were sneaking around with one of the Reds?" In the beat of Saba's startled, guilty silence, Iracena smirked. "That woman you were with. Nazeya mes Akhal, right?" Saba could only stare at her. "Maybe you shouldn't be so high and mighty."

"Perhaps you can explain to me how sitting in the middle of a crowded pub, in full view of more than a hundred people, counts as sneaking."

"Does Alvana know?"

Oh, that was the last fucking straw.

"You know what," Saba said. "There's no need for you to come to rehearsal tomorrow morning. Or any morning." She sounded calmer than she felt. Her nerves had already been frayed to threads before this; her pulse was fluttering like a bird in her throat. "You're done."

"Seriously?" There was a laugh around the edges of Iracena's voice.

"Yes. You don't get to set my friends against me, you don't get to nose into my personal affairs, and you don't get to pretend you're better than the other Lights. You're more trouble than you're worth, and I don't have to endure you."

Iracena's jaw tightened and she stood. "If you'll excuse me, then."

"You're so very excused." She only relaxed when Iracena had stormed out of the bar. Talesyn's teeth and tongue, what a day. She needed another drink.

~

Alvana cried when Saba told her that she'd fired Iracena—tears of frustration that one more thing had gone wrong in this dreadful, tedious, exhausting year of things going wrong. It was like being pinned to the floor of a bar in the middle of a fight and slapped over and over. And over.

They were all tired, but Alvana was wearing down in a way that didn't sit well with Saba—she was getting grey and sometimes she didn't cry at all. And there'd been no ink on her fingertips for a week or more. She wasn't writing.

Something had to be done, and there weren't many options—Saba was living on a shoestring budget already, scraping through on the scanty theater profits. When the audiences didn't come, it was Saba's pay that got cut first.

They needed new material. It would be far from prudent to hire a translator just on the off chance that the Mangarha book by the famous poet might contain something useful that could lift Alvana's spirits, when that money might be required for rent, or food, or... Well, court fees.

Nazeya's offer hung in the back of her mind like a windchime, tinkling gently every now and then with the passing breeze.

Two weeks later, she found herself on the doorstep of the mes Akhal bookshop just as the streetlamps were being lit. She fiddled and fidgeted with the contents of her pockets and told herself firmly that she'd go inside. Soon. Any moment now.

"Saba?"

Fuck. She cleared her throat and turned—Nazeya, of course, that voice couldn't be anyone's but hers. "Good evening."

She was lovely in lamplight too—she wore a simple Avaren-style dress of green-blue today, the deep and strange color of the sky at dusk. Her glossy hair was braided, wrapped around her head like a crown. "Ah, this is my family's shop," Nazeya said awkwardly, almost apologetic.

"Yes, I came to see you." She cleared her throat, removed her hat to be polite. Cleared her throat again. "Uh. Market day, was it?" she said, glancing down at the basket hooked over Nazeya's elbow.

"Just a few things for dinner. Why did you come to see me?"

"The book. The Mangarha book that we talked about before."

"Yes? What about it?"

Saba's voice failed. She tried again. "Would you still be interested in translating it?" Nazeya nodded slowly, brightening; it only made Saba more nervous. "About payment..."

"None necessary. I insist."

"I'm insisting too."

"Then I'll take my payment in trade."

"Trade?"

"A couple evenings of you helping me run lines."

"Yes," Saba blurted. "Yes. I'd be—delighted." She suppressed a wince.

"Would you? Even though it would be benefiting the Reds?"

It would be benefiting you, Saba thought. She rallied enough to give Nazeya a rake's smile. "Do you expect me to pass up an opportunity to recite with a pretty girl? It's as compelling for me as that book is for you."

Nazeya's eyes sparkled just before she looked away. "Good, then we agree the trade is fair." The smile had not entirely faded from her face. "When would you like to start?"

"Tomorrow? My rooms?"

Nazeya considered a moment. "Yes, I think that would be best. It wouldn't do for us to be seen in public together. And..." She glanced at the shop and smiled wryly. "I'd rather not have my family hanging over our shoulders."

"I'm not sure what to make of this," Nazeya said, laying her pen down. There was only one chair, so Saba was lounging sideways in bed, leaning back against the wall and penciling notes on one of the other dusty old plays they'd scraped out of Alvana's box of files.

"What is it?" she said.

Nazeya shook her head. "It's archaic, and it's been a long time since I spoke much Mangarha; there's a few words I'll have to ask my grandmother about. But I have the gist of it and I..." She frowned at the book.

"What, a hoax? Not a real copy of *Two Moons and Twelve Stars*?"

"I don't know. It's strange."

"Well, I don't care either way, as long as there's something useful in there." She snapped her mouth closed. "Ignore that last thing. I didn't say that."

"I'm not an idiot," Nazeya said mildly. "Of course you're looking for a play, or at least the bones of one." She rubbed one of the pages between her fingers. "Thing is... I don't know. The binding's been replaced. Do you know anything about bookbinding?"

"Nothing."

"The pages are better quality than the binding is. Fine antique vellum—but it's bound in pasteboard and cloth."

"And?"

"And so I think this book might be older than it looks at first glance. You see re-binding all the time, that's not odd—but it's a little strange to put a cheap binding on a book this nice."

"But someone did. Why?"

"Maybe they thought selling the cover and text separately was more profitable. Or maybe it was damaged and the owner couldn't afford a perfect replacement. I couldn't say." She flicked through the pages. "But it's written in an antiquated form of the women's hand..." She paused, and Saba nearly swooned—*that* was the kind of pause she had been trying to beat into the new players' heads for the last few weeks. "It's not what I was told *Two Moons and Twelve Stars* was like as a text. That's what the title says, and there are a few poems that sound familiar, but there's too many."

"Reverse attribution, maybe? A lesser poet selling their work under the name Erhabar?"

"Or several poets. My father told me that *Two Moons and Twelve Stars* consists of two longer works and twelve shorter ones of varying lengths—he said it's an assembled collection of selected pieces from Erhabar's body of work, and that no two editions are the same. This is... dozens and dozens of poems, perhaps hundreds, and several long works—essays, memoirs, fictional stories, and what seems to be commentary. I've only skimmed bits of it, but... Here, look at this. In Mangarha, a poem often looks like this." She handed one of her pages of notes to Saba. The text was neatly written in an almost perfect square in the center of the page. "It's a little misformed because naturally the words are different lengths in Avaren. And, well, anyone can tell you what commentary looks like."

She handed Saba another page, filled with regular lines of text with paragraph breaks, like any letter or novel. "And this seems pretty self-evident as well." Another page—short lines, each one labeled at the beginning with a name. Brief descriptions of actions. A paragraph-long section of text in the middle, set off in brackets.

Saba's eyes swept across it and said with no little surprise, "A play." It was only through great care that she kept the tension from her voice.

"A play. There are several."

"By Erhabar?" Saba asked.

"I... don't think so. I'm not sure who they're by. The scribe seems to be commenting on them, rather than making a fair copy. In that section, she's ranting about the decisions the characters are making. She seems to be upset that the whole plot of the play hinges on the characters' unwillingness to communicate their problems to each other."

"Mmm," said Saba sagely. "I approve. Madam Scribe and I understand each other. So she's commenting on someone else's play, which she's copied down into this book?"

"I'm not sure. She's using some odd pronouns and a politeness system that's very strange to my ear—I *think* it's the intimate-informal second person, but I'm not sure what the implications of that are, whether she's talking to herself, or if the play was written by another person... If it's all right with you, I'd like to ask my grandmother about it."

Saba hesitated. "Only her? You swear it?"

"By the boards and backdrops," Nazeya said seriously. "I'll translate the rest of this play for you as soon as I can—I know it's not one of Alvana's, but... Well, I hope it helps a little."

"What if they're all *bad* plays that Madam Scribe only wrote down so she could tear them apart?"

"Why would she have done that?" Nazeya asked softly, looking at the pages before her. "In such a beautiful book, why would she have spent the vellum and ink to do that? Judge it on its own merits, when I've finished. If it's good, perform it."

"Forgive me if I don't get emotionally attached. Wouldn't bringing Yermekov a free play get you in her good graces?"

Nazeya gave her a gently hurt look; Saba subsided, the rest of whatever catty comments she'd been about to make dying in her throat.

There was a long silence before Nazeya said softly, "I don't blame you for not trusting me."

"I want to," Saba replied, just as quiet. "But I don't know yet if I want to let myself. Everyone knows my weakness for gorgeous women. Even I admit to it."

"I wish you wouldn't say things like that."

Saba looked away and cleared her throat. "Ah. Sorry. Is it comments on your looks that you don't like?"

"Partially."

"Consider it unsaid, then, with my apologies." Saba took a breath. "I did say I have a weakness. Out of curiosity, why— well. No, I suppose I don't need to ask. A moment's thought was enough to figure it out."

"Why I don't like it when people tell me I'm pretty?"

"Because everyone says so, as if there's nothing else about you worthy of comment or admiration?"

"Just so. It gets rather tiring."

"No need to understate it," Saba said mildly.

"It has long since become excruciating," Nazeya amended. "Thank you, you're quite right." After a moment, she added with a bitter, wry smile, "Verity and Zitka didn't have any comments on my audition, you know, when I first read for them. They bickered with each other, right in front of me, about whether I had the right look to play the part. Whether I was too pretty for it."

"I'm sorry."

"I liked that about you, you know, even after you'd shattered my hero-worship. You thought the most important thing about me was how well I'd played Cosima."

"It was. It is."

Nazeya looked away again, smiling. They said nothing more, and in a few minutes Nazeya gathered up her things and the book, and said goodnight.

～

Fifteen days after that first conversation in Saba's flat, she received a very brief note summoning her to the mes Akhal bookshop. She went under cover of darkness, as instructed, and Nazeya met her at the door. "Grandmother and I have been looking at the book. We might have something for you."

"Oh?" said Saba, shucking off her coat as she followed Nazeya up the back stairs. "What do you have?"

"Provenance."

The word seemed to send a tremor through the room, rattling the windowglass faintly. "Provenance," Saba said, as Nazeya opened the door and gestured her through.

"We're not completely sure, but—"

"Bah!" said an extraordinarily old woman sitting at a table. "We're mostly sure."

"My grandmother, Rayyana mes Akhal," Nazeya said. "Grandmother, this is Mistress Sabajan Hollant, who owns the book."

Rayyana's nod to her was both dignified and dismissive. Saba mentally admired it and tucked it away in her mental catalogue of performable character tics. "Very pleased to meet you, grandmother," Saba said in Khagri.

"May your own mother and grandmother rest peacefully in the lap of the gods," Rayyana said. "They *must* be dead, to let you go around with an accent that bad."

"Sorry," Nazeya whispered with a wince, pulling another chair up to the table.

Saba took it, studying Rayyana with delighted curiosity and trying not to mimic her posture and gestures overmuch. "Provenance, you said, grandmother?" she said, now in Avaren.

Rayyana sniffed. "I was a scholar when I was young, back in the old country. Once, my teacher took us to the king's house of treasures. You pay a coin and you can look at all the wonderful things he owns, sitting in glass cases with guards to watch them. I'm almost certain this book was one of them."

Saba blinked down at the cloth-and-pasteboard bound book on the table, drab and unassuming. "You recognize it? How? Nazeya said the cover had been replaced."

"Because I'm a bookbinder's daughter, girl." Rayyana picked it up and turned it edgewise. "The headband." She tapped the colorful band that anchored the stitching at the spine—it *was* distinctive, now that Saba noticed it. "And the stitching." Rayyana held the book open to the center of a folio of pages and showed a line of vibrant purple stitching. The threads shone in the light, more brilliant even than silk. "Sea-wich thread, and cochineal dye. This is a king's book."

Saba opened and closed her mouth several times. "Nazeya said there were too many poems."

Rayyana snorted. "Nazeya was never a good student, never listened to lessons." Nazeya ducked her head and folded her hands tight in her lap. "*Two Moons and Twelve Stars* is a Mangarha classic, but copies of it are *always* abridged. Can you blame them?" She gestured at the book. "No one would buy something like this. No one wants to write all this out by hand—now that we have all these newfangled print shops, perhaps we'll see complete copies—*maybe*. An abridged copy typically consists of two of the long works and some assortment of twelve of the poems. This," she put her hand flat on the book, 'Is one of the only complete volumes in existence. *Two Moons and Twelve Stars* isn't the name of the book, it's the name of the first poem, a near-epic of awkward length—longer than an essay, not long enough to be a book itself. Unfortunately, not one of the good ones. Erhabar used some," Rayyana sniffed derisively, "*experimental* literary devices in that one."

"And the plays?"

"She was no playwright. But her royal patrons had a taste for them, much as we do today, so she did what Nazeya and I are doing now—translations. They are included here in what can be considered her complete works."

"Who was she translating?" Saba asked.

Rayyana and Nazeya exchanged a glance. Nazeya went to a writing desk in the corner, unlocked one of the drawers, removed a thick sheaf of papers, and handed them to Saba.

Saba took it. "*The Trials of Polyphontes.* That's an Oissic name, isn't it?" She frowned. "When did Erhabar live, do you know?

"Born in the fifth year of the Golden Dynasty," Rayyana said. "And died in the sixty-eighth. By the Avaren calendar, the years 337 to 405."

A truly insane thought passed through Saba's head... No. It couldn't be. Could it?

Nazeya added quietly, "Grandmother translated the commentary on *Polyphontes* too. It sounds like the playwright was a contemporary of Erhabar's—she refers to it as a newer play brought over from the east country, which is what people in Mangar-Khagra used to call Oissos."

"Not a lot of Oissic playwrights in the mid-300s," Saba muttered. Her hands were faintly trembling. "At least, not a lot whose work has survived." Her lungs were burning. She hadn't breathed in several moments. "It's probably nothing."

Nazeya said, low and urgent, "No. You know what that could be."

"I know it is probably nothing," Saba said, folding up the play and stuffing it down the front of her doublet. "Grandmother Rayyana, thank you for all your work. I must excuse myself."

She'd bolted halfway down the stairs before Nazeya caught up with her. "Saba!"

Saba stopped abruptly, turned back to her. Her mind was racing. "We may still be able to make some use of it, even if it's nothing."

"*Saba.*"

"Things are more often nothing than they are something."

"Saba," Nazeya said again, frustrated.

"Maintaining a healthy skepticism hurts no one." She reached out and tucked a lock of hair behind Nazeya's ear before she could stop herself. "I'd rather be ecstatic and wrong than disappointed and wrong. Wouldn't you?"

"I'd rather have hope," Nazeya said. "Wouldn't *you*?"

"Not false hope. Not premature hope, hatched before it had the strength to live in the world. Peace, chickadee. Alvana knows more than anyone about this stuff. I'll entrust it to her judgment."

~

Saba threw herself into the comfortable chair in Alvana's rooms. Alvana herself was already nose-deep in the pages Saba had shoved at her, and she sank down onto the other, more rickety chair, leaning her elbow on the desk beneath the window.

"*The Trials of Polyphontes*," she murmured. "That's a Oissic name. Where did you get this?"

"A book from your father." Saba clasped her hands

between her knees and sat forward. "But the author of the book, Suri Erhabar, didn't write this one."

"Mm," said Alvana, brow furrowed as she read. "This will have to be polished."

"Translator not much of a poet?"

"It just needs some tinkering. The words should *sing*." She turned the page. "Working in translation is always a challenge. You remember when I did, uh..." She snapped her fingers a few times.

"Ludo Genehofen, *The Winds of Walebruck*. Yes, vividly."

Alvana paused and frowned. "Wait, you said Erhabar didn't write this?"

"No. She got it from someone in Oissos. A friend. I'm assuming it must have been a very popular play, to go to the trouble." Saba took a breath. "Erhabar lived in the mid-300s. Died in early 400s."

Alvana's face went very pale, then two spots of color came high on her cheeks as she looked up sharply at Saba. Her hands shook so hard the pages rattled. "Saba," she said, and Saba took another deep, steadying breath.

"Yeah. So... you think?"

Alvana looked down at the pages again. "Did you read this?"

"Not all of it. Enough to know that you should see it. Did you see the commentary?"

"Y-yes. She—" Alvana swallowed. "Look. Look, right here. 'My dear friend Kyra', it says. Kyra, who... who wrote it and sent her a copy as a gift." Alvana's free hand covered her mouth—she was still trembling all over.

"And in almost seven hundred years, no one took any notice of that name," Saba whispered. "Because the university at Mytea was only unearthed from the volcanic ash fifty years ago. The records. The faculty rolls."

Alvana looked at her. Her eyes were filled with tears, her

nose already blotchy. "A playwright named Kyra, a contemporary of Erhabar," she said, her voice trembling. "Like... Like Kyra Palustrasos of the University of Mytea, who *also* lived from the mid-300s to the early 400s and—and until fifty years ago was only remembered with her penname..."

"Euhemenon," they whispered together.

Alvana's eyes were wild. "If it's a fake, it's a very elaborate fake."

"We have a vague provenance on the original text. If my translator's memory is true, it belonged to the king of Mangar-Khagra. Which..."

"Oh fuck. Lord of Poets, lend me light. We have a *lost Euhemenon play.*"

"And we tell *no one.*"

"What about your translator?"

"Don't worry about her." A heavy weight settled in her stomach—she was lying. Only by omission, certainly, but... this was Alvana, her first friend, her best friend.

"We can't speak of this. We can't let anyone know we have it."

"The girls have to learn their lines. But no, no details about it outside this room."

Alvana's eyes filled with tears. "Saba, what are we going to do?"

"Goodness, woman, what's the matter?" Saba cried. "This is a wonderful thing! A gift from our *best bro* Clevertongue himself! He might as well have handed it to us directly and said, 'Sorry about all the nonsense, ladies! Actually, you were my real favorites all along!'"

"If—if Dauren and Yermekov find out—"

"We'll keep it from them. I promise. I *promise.* This time we'll do it right. We won't tell the troupe that it's a Euhemenon play. They know I just bought a nothing play from that country bumpkin last week. We'll tell them it's his, right up until the day before we perform it, when we stand in front of the audience and say *come back tomorrow and see a Euhemenon play that's been lost for near a thousand years.*"

Alvana wiped her eyes with the palms of her hands. "Lie to them, you mean."

The weight roiled in Saba's stomach. "No, just fail to tell them one hundred percent of the truth. We'll tell them ninety percent of the truth. It's that or fight off possibly *literal* assassins from Yermekov and Dauren, which is what I'd do if *they* had a new Euhemenon play. Surely it's not so bad to tell ten percent of a lie if it's to keep our family safe. And we'll be subtle—just slip in a scene or two here and there during rehearsals, like any other nothing play that we're not thrilled about. We can have them up to speed in another three weeks, I'd say, and we'll have it." She chewed on her thumbnail absently. "In the meantime... We could hire Enryn to keep it in his breast pocket?"

"He's forbidden from being involved in any fights," Alvana said, propping her head in her hands, elbows on the desk. "It isn't fair to endanger his freedom like that."

"Hm," said Saba. "Keep it at your father's place—no. No, that won't work. He's too gullible, bless him."

"Another lawyer? A real one? Surely the Lord Chancellor has a solicitor he uses, or can get a recommendation from someone."

Saba groaned. "He'll just snap at us because it's not one of *your* plays."

Alvana sniffled away the last of her tears. "Well, I don't have any other ideas, so you'd better pick whichever is the right one."

Saba tapped her fingers more frantically on the arm of the chair. "I'll keep it for now. If all else fails, I'll resign myself to asking Lord Chancellor for his help." She slumped back in the chair. "I suppose he *is* the one person not in the troupe who we can trust to keep a secret. Y'know, since it hugely benefits him and so on."

~

Three days later, Saba was busily taking inventory of all the old costumes—mostly masks and hats; you could do a shocking amount with the right mask or hat—when Artagne found her.

"We have a problem," Artagne said urgently, her mouth set in a grim line.

"What else is new?" Saba grunted from behind a huge armful of slightly moth-eaten secondhand finery. "We don't have *a* problem, we have dozens of problems. Ugh, was this dress always so dowdy?"

Artagne seized her arm, spilling the costumes onto the floor, and spun her around. "Alvana's been arrested."

~

"On what charges?" Saba said as they flew down the stairs through the back of the theater.

"I don't know for sure," Artagne said, hurrying behind her. "Debt? No one knows! I just stopped in at the coffee-house to buy lunch and the owner asked me if we were going to be all right!"

They hit the main floor and dove through the stage doors and out into the open. Saba ignored the steps and jumped directly down into the yard. "Saba!" one of the others cried, but she charged across the sawdust, up the opposite stairs, and out through the front doors.

Her mind whirled—where was Alvana? Where would they take her? Was she already in a cell somewhere?

One thought made her pause: Alvana wouldn't be in debt. She had money of her own. Not heaps of it; that was why she lived in a one-room flat in a boarding house. She had no vices —she drank only occasionally and always sparingly; she was too savvy and too compulsively cautious to fall for any investment schemes, whether legitimate or otherwise; she knew she was terrible at games of chance and avoided them so ardently that Saba could only wile her into a simple game of knacks-and-dodgers if there were no stakes but bragging rights; she celebrated the Feast of Temptations every year by going to *bookstores* and *fancy pen shops.*

So what in the world could she have done to get herself arrested?

Unless...

There was a particular thing that street illusionists did, and Saba hated them for it—they gestured with one hand and worked their tricks with the other, so that you were watching the wrong place when the so-called *magic* happened. The card vanished or reappeared, the blue ball beneath the cup turned green, the handkerchief blossomed into a dove and exploded from their hands in a thunder of wings.

Wherever Alvana was, she could probably take care of herself. She had resources at her disposal, not least of which was that big beautiful brain.

So what *wasn't* Saba supposed to be looking at?

"Alvana's flat," she growled.

Saba scoured the flat from the rafters to the floorboards.

She did not know whether or not to be terrified that she couldn't find the Euhemenon play—there was nothing out of place, and it did not *seem* that anyone had searched before her... Alvana could have found a very good hiding spot for it, or she could have it safe on her own person. "Oh shit, Talesyn, *please,*" she found herself whispering frantically as she searched. "Lord of Poets, Song-spinner, you fucking *know* I'm yours, so you'd better fucking come through for me and mine on this one. *Fuck.* Clevertongue, Lorelord, Silverthroat, *please.*"

Just to be safe, Saba gathered up every other scrap of Alvana's writing that she could find, packed them into a small chest, and hauled it out to the street. She scuttled through the back alleys, glancing nervously over her shoulder the whole way until she reached a neighborhood where she could find a hired carriage. She hailed the first one she saw and paid the extortionate fee to be taken across town to the Grand Chancery.

Upon alighting from the carriage, she hauled her burden onto her shoulder, braced herself, glanced up at the golden-brick facade of the huge building, and walked in the front door. There at the desk in the first room was her old friend, that irritating clerk.

"Hi," said Saba. "Good to see you again. I need to see the Lord Chancellor, if he's got a minute."

"Would you indeed," the clerk said, eyeing her rather tired breeches, her entire lack of hosen or doublet, her loose sweat-stained shirt... Thank the gods she'd been wearing shoes when Artagne had come up, or Saba would have bolted out the door barefoot. "The Lord Chancellor is not a man to whom petitions can be made directly, madam. I'm sure you understand."

"He'll want to see me."

"You'll have to remind me what your business with him is. After last time, I'd rather scrubbed it from my memory."

Saba gave him a flat look. "I'm in charge of his theater troupe. My business with him is *about* his theater troupe."

"Oh yes," he said, wrinkling his nose. "A player."

"There is currently a danger to his investment. You might as well go tell someone it's me. I'll wait here. You can tell him I apologize for not making an appointment in advance, but it's urgent."

～

"Madam Hollant," said the Lord Chancellor from around a mouthful of chicken. "What a surprise."

"Your Lordship. Thank you for your time. You appreciate brevity, do you not?"

He nodded, still chewing, and gestured for her to continue.

She set the chest of Alvana's writing at her feet and clasped her hands behind her back. "I know that your rivalry with the Lord Seneschal is as keen as ours is with his players. I have reason to believe that the Lord Seneschal's Women are again attempting to sabotage us. Alvana Stillgrail has just been arrested."

"And you think it's that bastard's quaint little troupe."

Saba was torn between the cozy glow of shared dislike and the sting that came from catching part of the insult. "That's the prevailing theory. I need your help."

"Madam Hollant, I hardly have time to bother with such petty matters as a childish squabble—theft of the play was one thing. That affected the entire company. But one single player of your troupe being arrested on charges which could very well be legitimate? Sort it out amongst yourselves."

"You hired us *because* of Alvana!"

"I hired you because she wouldn't write for any other troupe in the city."

"She can't write at all if she's in jail!"

The Lord Chancellor rolled his eyes. "You're being rather hysterical about all this. Being in jail isn't going to stop her from writing. Perhaps she'll benefit from it. No distractions."

"But if they've accused her of something entirely false—is

the Lord Seneschal above such petty swipes? Would he stoop to shaming you by discrediting and disbanding your troupe one by one, starting with the writer?"

"He might," the Lord Chancellor admitted, grudgingly.

"Sir, I ask for a kernel of faith. We have something that will blow the Lord Seneschal and his Players clear off the map." Unless it had already been stolen. "In five years, no one will even remember their names."

The Lord Chancellor raised his eyebrow and took another bite of his lunch. "Is that right?"

"We have..." Saba paused in just the way she was always trying to teach her newcomers, "a new Euhemenon play."

To her confounded dismay, he crinkled his nose. "Don't care for Euhemenon plays. Do something else."

"Sir! A *new* Euhemenon play! One which has been lost for a thousand years!"

"So? I don't care for her work. I've seen several, and I find them tiresome. *Thera and Kliode, Caelavius*... They rather put me to sleep."

"But a *new* one, your lordship! It's like discovering a new continent!"

"I think most people don't care for Euhemenon," he went on, chewing pensively. "Other than scholars and players. And the Lord Seneschal, but his flaws are manifold. Not really a playwright for the common folk, Euhemenon. I'd much rather have a new Stillgrail play." He shot her a sharp look. "There *will* be a new Stillgrail play this season, will there not?"

"Not if she's in prison," Saba said.

The Lord Chancellor tsked and pushed his plate away. "You're really quite fixated on this, aren't you? I know writers; most of them can write just as well in one empty little room as they can in another."

Saba gritted her teeth. "She's working on a new play now, but writing takes time and we have to perform *something*. We need new material, *good* material, and we need the cash flow to pay for it. Otherwise, I'll have to buy cheap shit off some nobody from the country—his father probably a basketweaver or a glovemaker or something."

"If you're asking for money, I decline."

"I'm not, your lordship. I'm just saying that it's not sustainable to simply repeat the crowd favorites over and over again. We have to do the Euhemenon play. No one's going to say they don't like it in public, anyway. Makes them look uncultured."

"I said it."

"You can afford to, of course."

"I want a Stillgrail play."

"You will get it," Saba said desperately. "Of course you will."

"I'm not paying for anything besides that."

"And Alvana?"

He sighed and pushed his plate away.

"She can't write if she's in prison," Saba said, a touch more severely. "Really, she can't. At least help me find out what the charges are."

"Fine," he said, cold.

Saba was banished to the entrance hall while the Lord Seneschal sent a runner out to the watchhouse. She sat on the chest, fidgeting and tapping her fingertips against the beaten wood for nearly two hours, avoiding the eyes of the awful clerk at the desk. At regular intervals she shot off the chest and rummaged through the papers to make sure, once again, that the copies of the Euhemenon play were not amongst them.

Again and again, they were not.

The runner returned about the same time that Saba's

stomach was really beginning to pang with hunger. He gave a note to the clerk, who swept past her without a glance and let himself into the Lord Chancellor's chambers. Saba was called in a few minutes later.

"I really didn't have time for this today," the Lord Chancellor said, now entirely icy. "What did you think you were playing at?"

"Pardon?"

"I have a note from the chief constable," he said, pushing a piece of paper across the desk to her with two fingers. "Alvana Stillgrail is being held in the Basko Street watch house. She was arrested last night for breaking and entering."

"*What?* No, there must be some mistake. Alvana wouldn't. She just wouldn't."

"Wouldn't she?" He said, withering. "I told you I wanted no more petty scandals, and then Alvana Stillgrail herself, the *reason* I'm patronizing your troupe at all, commits a serious criminal offense."

"Whose house is she supposed to have—"

"Zitka Yermekov's!" Lord Chancellor roared, surging to his feet; Saba flinched. He planted his hands on the desk and leaned forward. "Don't think you can play me for a fool, madam! You knew about this."

"My lord! By my honor, I swear I didn't!"

"Your honor isn't worth stable dirt to me!" His voice fell back to an icy calm: "I will not have my name associated with low criminals, especially after the events of last year. I withdraw my patronage."

Gods, Saba longed to walk out. Let him withdraw his support. Let him. He hadn't done anything for them. They could go back to being the Lights, they could perform whatever they liked... But if Alvana were really imprisoned, if she were found guilty (which she could be, whether or not the charges were true), then everything would be over. This was one situation where a noble patron could, in fact, be useful.

"My lord, please. This is either a misunderstanding, or someone has conspired to have Alvana falsely accused. There is no way she would have ever done such a thing, none!" He glared, cold and unblinking. "The Euhemenon play—I know you don't like her—"

"I don't."

"I know. But this is—this is something which historians will write about. And I, personally," Saba said, drawing on every ounce of acting she had within her, "I want them to write that the first new Euhemenon play in a thousand years was discovered, adapted, and performed by *The Lord Chancellor's Players*. That's something to be remembered. That's something that the Lord Seneschal can't ever beat. That's a *legacy*, my lord."

"Get out."

"My lord, *please*!"

He did not tell her again. She could think of nothing more to say that would get him to listen, so she hauled Alvana's trunk of papers onto her shoulder and left.

"Alvana, what the fuck *happened*?"

Though her cheeks were tear-streaked, Alvana's expression was stony. She said nothing. The Basko Street watch house was cool inside, its thick stone walls blocking out the late spring warmth.

Saba put her head in her hands. "Alvana. Don't be like this. I'm fucking desperate here. How on earth did you get arrested for breaking into Yermekov's rooms?"

Alvana sniffed. "They caught me."

"Seven gods and a pint of beer, woman! Doing *what*?"

"Stealing from her," said Alvana, without a lick of regret.

"You too, traitor?" Saba screeched. She seized the bars of Alvana's cell and wrung them, being unable to reach Alvana's neck. "Between you and the idiot men, I might as well resign myself to dying in squalor! I'll sit on the streetcorners with a ratty old blanket around my shoulders, reciting monologues from *Caelavius* and Stillgrail for coins! All the urchins will say, 'That's old lady Hollant, that is! Me da says she was once the finest player in the city! Oi, let's go steal her shoes and see how many fancy insults she can spit at us! Last week she called me a waterlogged dog-strumpet, she did!' And it'll be because of *shit like this*."

Alvana lifted her chin, stubborn. "I wasn't taking anything but what already belonged to me."

"Oh shit," Saba breathed. "The plays?"

Embarrassment flickered briefly across Alvana's face and was subsumed once more by stubbornness. "No. I was going to get Handsome."

"I beg your fucking pardon, you were getting *what*?"

"Handsome."

Saba stared blankly at her. "Sweetheart, you're gonna have to give me a little more—"

"My *puppy*. You *met* him."

"When did you ever have a puppy?" Saba screeched.

"When I was with Zitka!" Alvana snapped in reply.

Saba pinched the bridge of her nose.

"I know you remember it," Alvana said with a scowl. "You were *there*."

"It's ancient history! That's what we're talking about, isn't it? That little love affair you and Yermekov had *eight fucking years ago*?"

"Yes."

Saba's voice rose several dozen octaves. "It lasted three

months! When did you get a dog? I remember *Yermekov* showing up with a dog one day—"

"*My* dog."

"*Where* did you get a dog?"

"My father gave him to us as a housewarming gift."

Saba paused. Subsided. "That does ring a bell."

"It should," Alvana said, furious tears welling in her flashing eyes. "Because I told you all about it when it happened, and I told you Zitka and I were arguing about his name, and then I cried because we'd been arguing ever since we moved in together, and you—you really don't remember any of this? Famous Sabajan Hollant, who has memorized a hundred plays, who remembers *everything?*"

"I don't remember everything! And I have to see something written down to really remember it! When were you telling me about all this? Where were we, what was I doing?"

"We were at the Theater of Truth—"

"So I was drunk."

Alvana hesitated. "I suppose you may have been a couple drinks in, yes."

Saba raised her eyebrows. She sat in her chair, crossed her legs, and laced her fingers over her knee. "What was it you were saying about the dog?"

"We fought over what to name him—he was *my* dog, *my* father gave him to me, *I* should have named him—and a week later, she left me and took—"

"Oh! Oh, *this* I remember! She took all your ink and paper, and you had a play to finish, but you were crying too hard to leave your room, so I had to go to the shops for you. She took a pair of earrings too, didn't she? And a few of your books?"

"And Handsome! He was mine! Zitka doesn't even like dogs!"

"Alvana, sweetheart, it was eight years ago."

"I've never forgiven her!" Alvana snarled.

Saba raised her hands. "Whoa there, settle down. Far be it from me to even faintly imply that you should forgive her, or indeed any Red. If you say the dog was yours, I believe you. Stealing someone's dog is a special kind of fucked up, and I retroactively hate Yermekov even more for it. She might as well be a war criminal! Handsome should have been like a nephew to me."

Alvana was beginning to sniffle again. Anger was not comfortable or natural for her, never had been—she was motivated by tears. Where Saba ended a hard cry feeling drained and exhausted, Alvana always came out the other side with energy and resolve. So this, this was a good sign.

"Like a nephew, I say!" Saba pressed on. "But darling, if you'd just told me, we could have gone together to fetch him back. We could have gone eight years ago! Why didn't you say anything?"

"Because it's silly, I know it's silly. You would've thought so."

"I beg your pardon, I most certainly would not! I love dogs! We could have taught him tricks and put him on stage, and everyone would have forgotten about the Reds in two seasons. What's he look like? Small dog, big dog?"

"Small side of medium," Alvana said, wiping her eyes with the heels of her hands. "Pointy ears, white and fluffy all over but for his little black feet."

"Sounds like Handsome was a good name for him," Saba said grandly. Fat tears spilled over Alvana's splotchy red cheeks. Good. Progress. "Why'd you wait so long to go after him?"

"I didn't," Alvana sobbed. "I've been trying to convince her to give him back to me *this whole time*."

Oh. Shit.

"I've written her letters. I've *begged*. She doesn't even like dogs, but she won't share him with me. She wouldn't even let me see him!"

Saba tightened her jaw. "That misbegotten bitch. Sweetheart, we're going to get him back, all right? I'll help you. Of course I'll help you. You should've known that I would."

Alvana buried her face in her hands.

"First, we'll get you out of here. I'll tell the Lord Chancellor what happened, and he'll get you a lawyer. All right?" He'd relent when he found out, surely. Saba was ninety percent sure the Lord Chancellor owned dogs himself. He'd understand *this*, of all things.

Alvana only nodded, wracked with silent sobs.

"Um," said Saba. "About the play, though..."

"It's in my apartment. Both of them are—I'm nearly finished with the new one," Alvana said, and Saba's heart stuttered.

"Where in your apartment, dear heart?"

"Left side of my fireplace. There's a loose brick."

Relief staggered her. "I didn't look there. I swept up all the papers I could find into a box and left it with Artagne at the theater before I came here."

Alvana took one shuddering breath after another. "Better go get it. If someone else looks—"

"Leave it to me."

～

Saba flew back across the city on foot—she'd spent all but her last few pennies bribing the watch to let her see Alvana. Her heart pounded in her chest like Lord Ystrac of the Greenwood himself was hunting her, like he was bringing to bear upon her all the inescapable wilderness-fear of trapped prey. If she hadn't been running flat out, she wouldn't have even dared to breathe. The two plays were her only thought. The plays, the plays.

All consciousness vanished, returning with a jolt only when she was in Alvana's flat and already had her hands on the bricks of the fireplace, fumbling around blindly to find the loose one—there.

And inside—

Paper.

She sagged against the wall, hand to her chest, and wheezed with relief.

Everything else could be dealt with. They had the plays.

She made herself stand still for all of two excruciating minutes, her heart slowing, her breath evening out.

Right, next thing on the list: Avenging Alvana.

Saba charged through the streets, stoking her fires until she felt as though she should be taking up twice the space that she did.

Scarlet rhymes with harlot, Saba mused to herself as she strode up to the forecourt of the Red Theater. *Must mention that to Alvana. She'll make it clever.*

"Come one, come all!" shouted the crier at the theater door. "By popular demand, a performance of Yermekov and Dauren's greatest masterpiece, *Some By Virtue Fall*! One penny at the door! Just one penny to break your heart! You'll tell your children and grandchildren about this day!"

Saba seethed. Of course. Of course, today of all days.

She paid her penny and disappeared into the crowd of groundlings in the yard—being solidly shorter than average, it was easier to hide there than it would be in the galleries. Still, she wished she had a hat with a brim she could pull down, or a hood to hide her face.

The Red Theater was of comparable size to the Lights,

though their stage was deeper where the Lights' was wider, and the spire atop the roof of their heavens was not quite as high. The greasy scent of sausages filled the air, winding in between that of the masses of groundlings.

A trumpet blast—Saba's heart leapt into her throat.

First, the dedication: A brief verse in honor of Talesyn Songspinner, Lord of the Light of Poetic Inspiration, that he might stand amongst the audience and be pleased by his players, that he might stand beside the players and bestow his audience with a glimpse of glory.

Then Chorus set the scene, a trio of young women who (unlike some people Saba might mention) knew how to project their damn voices to the very back of the hall. The crowds settled, stilled as much as such a crowd could. Alvana's words filled the theater like wine filling a cup—if Saba closed her eyes she could almost believe that they were still Alvana's words. She mouthed along with them silently. Every line.

Enter Aucien, played by Zitka Yermekov herself, the bitch. Fie upon her. Her golden hair was plaited back into a long rope that reached nearly to her hips, and her blue velvet doublet was a wonder of embroidery, flashing in the sunlight as she gesticulated, one hand resting on the jeweled pommel of a sword slung at her hip. She looked like a *prince*, and she carried herself with a quiet dignity that only made Saba want to punch her across her damn face—she was better as Aucien than she'd been as the Lord of Temptation.

Then, soon after, Cosima's entrance (Verity Dauren, rather than Nazeya—the Reds didn't like to commit one player to just one part). For swathes and swathes of glorious iambs, she and Aucien embraced, plotted, beguiled, and plotted some more.

The play tumbled on. It jarred Saba to hear the music of Alvana's language so corrupted and *wronged*. Every mistimed pause, every incorrect emphasis grated against her like claws down her back.

The masquerade, the secret plan, the uncertainty—Aucien wondering if Cosima had betrayed him; Cosima wondering the same of him.

And then.

Then.

Who dares call me, Saba mouthed along with the Lord of Temptation, and—her eyes flew open, and her stomach dropped sharply.

Iracena.

Iracena du Cassa, upgraded from the role of Orchilo, gentleman blowhard, to—to *Saba's* role.

The rest of the monologue was lost to Saba's ears, as if swallowed up by the white sound of rushing water. Iracena acted the Lord of Temptation from the crotch, as Saba had done, but *not* as Saba would have done it. Her movements were too stiff and unfamiliar, and she wore the huge codpiece like it was just cloth and straw or rags, not like it was real, engorged flesh straining in its hunger for the world.

"Fie on you!" Saba's voice thundered out of her, seizing easy dominance over Iracena's. "Crossed and cursed! Faithless cows! Dishonorable!" Ripples ran through the audience, and Iracena stumbled to a halt on the stage—Saba thrilled with vicious, spiteful triumph. *She* would never have stopped in the middle of that monologue, no matter who heckled her from the yard. "Witches and bitches, the lot of you!" she screamed again. "And Yermekov's a dog-fucker!"

She could hear a commotion behind her—that would be the theater's hired brawlers, coming to haul her off. "Face me like women, you shrieking fishwives! Yermekov! Would you have these people know you as a *coward*?"

Huge, brawny arms came around her at the waist and shoulder and one hand clapped over her mouth. She bit it hard, and its owner cursed and snatched it away, giving her just enough time to scream, 'Fight me! Yermekov, face me on the field of honor!" The rest was muffled in someone else's hand, this one padded with a filthy, smelly rag that made her choke. The arms around her were as tight and inflexible as barrel hoops; she couldn't even wriggle. They dragged her out amidst the jeers and cheers of the audience.

'Sabajan Hollant, my lords and ladies," came Yermekov's voice merrily from the stage. 'Another masterful performance from one of the shining stars of our fine city! Indeed, of all Avaris! Clap for her!"

The blood thundered in Saba's ears.

She was thrown bodily out of the theater. Before she had stopped tumbling heels-over-tits, the scarlet doors slammed closed. She sat up, covered in dirt and dust. Her face and arms and ribs were bruised, and her palms had been scratched raw by the cobblestones when she fell, not to mention a sundry collection of other small injuries which she was too angry to take stock of.

She was just pulling herself achingly to her feet when she heard steps coming around the side of the theater. Saba straightened up smartly, her aches vanishing into new fury.

Verity Dauren, still in her Cosima gown and glittering even brighter than Aucien, all red and white and gold. 'So," Dauren said, giving Saba's dishevelment a long, mocking up-and-down look. 'You challenged Zitka to a duel?"

'She'll take it if she's not a coward," Saba snarled.

'Surely you're not still carrying a grudge about the trial? As I recall, we won clean and fair."

'Neither clean nor fair. You wanted a fight—Yermekov did too. I've had enough. Enough, do you hear?" Saba spat at her feet. 'Need I insult you any louder? I shall declaim her into the *dirt* until she fights me."

Dauren twined a dark brown curl around one finger as she

regarded Saba. "As amusing and edifying as that no doubt would be, I have in fact been sent as envoy. Zitka accepts your challenge, and agrees to meet you on the field of honor three days hence, at dawn on Ystrac's Green."

"Fine. You're her second?"

"I am. And now I must away, madam, and prepare for my next scene." She smirked. "It's a terribly good play. Perhaps you'll get an opportunity to read the script sometime."

~

"A duel?" Artagne cried. "A duel! Saba, you imbecile, dueling is what got us into this mess in the first place!"

Saba stared into the middle distance and tried to look both very assured and nobly self-sacrificing. "I must do what I must do."

Artagne took her by the shoulders and shook her until her teeth rattled. "Sabajan Hollant!"

"Which one of you is best with a sword?" Saba said, wrenching herself away. "Tal?"

Artagne flung herself onto the steps from the yard to the stage and buried her face in her arms. "We're doomed! This is the end! Alvana imprisoned, Saba dead! No play, no support from our patron!"

"I won't *die*, calm down. Won't be arrested, either. Tal, you're my best swordsman, aren't you?"

Talsyn crossed his arms. "Why should I get involved in this? You made a fool of yourself in the middle of their play!"

"In the middle of *our* play that *they* stole," Saba said.

"In front of hundreds of people!"

"*Tal.* They've been thieves for nearly a decade—Yermekov stole Alvana's dog. This is a matter of honor."

"It's a matter of stupid."

"And *honor*. Are you with me or no?"

103

"Brassu's balls, fine," Talsyn groaned. "As long as Ishmeta doesn't object."

"Ask as soon as she gets back from the coffeehouse, and—"

The front doors of the theater creaked open; Saba looked up, expecting to see Ishmeta clothed in glory like a goddess of the coffeehouse, bearing her sacred symbols in each hand: a fresh steaming carafe and a pot of honey... But it was a runner in the Lord Chancellor's livery.

He trotted up to them. "Sabajan Hollant?"

"Yes," Saba said, her mouth dry. "Right here."

He handed her a small letter sealed with blue wax and the Lord Chancellor's crest, looked around the theater curiously, and left without another word. Tense with foreboding, Saba broke the wax, unfolded the letter, and skimmed it. "It's about Alvana." A moment later, she lowered her hands, felt the paper slip out of her suddenly numb fingers. "They're not releasing her. Her bail has been set at fifty princes." Her voice shook. "Fuck. She can't stay there awaiting trial. She can't. We have to get her out."

"With what money?" Talsyn asked flatly.

"Dig through your pockets!"

"Doesn't matter how many pockets we dig through," Inneo said. "We definitely don't have fifty princes. We'd have to sell off all the props and costumes to even get close. What about Papa Stillgrail? He's got loads of money."

"We can't tell him she's in trouble. He's getting old—his heart, the shock—Lady of Love, no, I can't be responsible for that decision. If we don't have the money, then we don't have it. I can ask Alvana if she wants to ask her father for it, but in the meantime, I have a duel to fight! And so does Tal!"

"Not," he said firmly, pointing a finger at her, "until my wife gets back and says it's fine."

The front door creaked open again to admit Ishmeta—yes, a goddess, just as Saba had envisioned: carafe in one hand, a little copper caddy holding honey- and cream-pots in the other. "Ishmeta, you are incandescent," Saba said before anyone else could get a word in, going at once to relieve Ishmeta of her burden. "Would you mind terribly if I borrowed Tal for a bit three days from now at dawn, for the purposes of showing those Red fucks who they're messing with?"

"If he wants to, sure," she replied easily.

"Ishmeta!" Talsyn roared, while Saba cackled under her breath and poured herself a cup of coffee. "You were supposed to say no!"

"Whatever for?"

"It's a duel!"

"You don't have to come if you don't want to, Tal," Saba said calmly, sipping her coffee. "But if something happens to me, there won't be anyone to back me up and the Reds win. It's up to you."

The morning was cool and dewy, the sun just obscured by a misty veil of cloud. Ystrac's Green was the only sacred park not marked with a full henge. In deference to the Wild Lord's preferences, it was thick with unmanicured trees and overgrown forest plants, a sprawl of wilderness in the middle of the city. Enryn, who held Ystrac second only to Idunet in his heart, had once told Saba that there was a a clearing and a great standing stone at the center of the Green. She, on the other hand, had never managed to make it very far past the edges before losing her nerve—even in bright noon sunshine or when the trees were alive with birdsong, it always seemed empty, alien, eerie.

Saba tapped her fingers restlessly against the hilt of the rapier at her belt. She rolled her shoulders. She flexed her off hand. She tried not to pace.

"This is stupid," Talsyn said behind her.

"Honor."

"Stupid."

"Should I take off my hat? Is it too much?"

"You're worried about your hat?"

Saba gestured emphatically to it—a jaunty tricorn with a purple satin cockade and a long white ostrich feather. It said *master duellist* in a way that Saba fancied, though she was beginning to have second thoughts. "Well?"

"It's fine," Talsyn said flatly. "It's possibly the most fine thing about your whole sartorial... situation. Either way, you'd better make a decision quick." He nodded down the forest path behind Saba. "By my head, here come our villains."

Saba looked over her shoulder—three horses and riders approaching. "Fuckers." The Reds had already seen her, and therefore they'd seen the hat. That was that, then. She shrugged off her half-cloak and tossed it to Talsyn, who draped it over one arm. Saba turned to meet the Reds, her hands on her hips. "What time do you call this?"

"I call it *on time*," Yermekov said, dismounting from her rose-grey mare. Saba eyed it suspiciously. A gift from the Lord Seneschal? Or was it simply that the Reds were so flush with coin after the success of the stolen play that they could afford to hire ponies for a morning jaunt? "What in the world are you wearing, Hollant?"

"Clothes," Saba said, adopting that annoying flat tone Talsyn had used to such effect.

"Mm," Yermekov said, as if there was something wrong with scarlet breeches, scarlet doublet, and a scarlet shirt. "Expecting to bleed today? Hoping to cover it up?"

"No." Shit. She should have gone with black.

"Already bleeding, then? It would have explained your grouchy mood in the theater the other day." Yermekov unstrapped her rapier from the saddle and unsheathed it.

'Shall we have our seconds determine the rules for us, or can we sort that out ourselves like women?"

Saba gritted her teeth. 'We fight to first blood."

Yermekov cast Saba's scarlets another glance. 'Mm. Anything else?"

'Yes. Let's make it interesting."

'A duel at dawn isn't already interesting enough? Does that explain the hat as well?" Yermekov's laughing eyes flicked up to her dramatic ostrich feather. 'How much makes it interesting for you, Hollant?"

'One hundred princes."

'Not a chance."

'Too rich for your blood?"

'When I win, you won't pay. You can't afford it."

'Fifty, then."

'You can't afford fifty, either," Dauren said.

'I can if we sell off all the props and costumes," Saba said flatly.

'Now there's a thought! Perhaps the hundred after all— you can sell off your theater too."

'Sabajan Hollant," Talsyn growled. 'Don't you fucking dare."

Saba muttered under her breath to him, 'If it's necessary, my will is hidden in the rafters of the costume room."

'Saba, this is stupid. Think about this."

'Nope." Saba drew her sword and turned on Yermekov.

'Fifty, then," Yermekov said, raising her sword and side-stepping into the interminable initial circling before the first blow, the testing of nerve and temper. They were players; the show was as habitual as breathing. 'I should mention how nice it is to see you, Sabajan. And how nice it was to see you at *our* play."

Saba twitched but didn't reply.

'I hope you'll come see more of them in the future. We'll

be reprising *Some by Virtue Fall* twice more this month. Maybe more. It does draw such a crowd! What a shame Alvana hasn't produced anything new in a while…"

Saba lunged; Yermekov easily parried.

"I was so hoping to come see something new and interesting at the Theater of Lights this season," Yermekov continued. "Have you noticed a strange smell, recently? I thought I did when I was walking past the other day. Perhaps the damp has gotten into your walls. Or perhaps the building is just as old—" Yermekov flicked the tip of her sword towards Saba, who knocked it aside, "—and tired— " Another strike, "—and mildewy as your plays."

Fire and rage seared along Saba's nerves. "Yermekov," she said in a low voice. "Let's change the terms of victory."

"To what?"

Saba wasn't, in point of fact, a great duellist. Neither was Yermekov, as far as she knew—with terms like "to first blood", it was a matter of luck rather than skill.

Saba didn't care about proving her luck was better.

I won't kill her, she mused. A few good strikes, though, enough to scare her—*that* was what she wanted. To make Yermekov as afraid of Saba as Saba was of her. To make her think twice about fucking with the Lights again. "Let's go until one of us yields. Unless you're afraid. I don't mind fighting delicately like maidens." Saba sketched a mocking bow. "If that's what the fair lady desires, I can be gallant."

She was ready to leap to the side when Yermekov took the opening and slashed at her. Saba recovered quickly and settled into Octem's first position—not that she'd had any formal training, but nearly every theater troupe kept a copy of Octem's *On Duelling* for reference.

They fought in earnest then, their swords flashing and clanging together in an almighty din that would've made better swordsmen cringe, until a line of cold fire traced across Saba's bicep. She cried out and clasped her hand to it.

Yermekov took two strides back, smirking, and examined the blade of her rapier. She wiped off a streak of Saba's blood with her thumb. "There's first blood," she said, breathless. "Care to yield, Hollant?"

Blood pounded in Saba's ears. "I'm not done yet."

"A shame," Yermekov said, stepping back to catch her breath. "You insist on making me humiliate you?"

"I sure as fuck do."

"One would have thought you'd be busy with more important matters than a duel. I've heard some rumors on the wind that you're *not* just a mildewy old tart after all."

"I heard those rumors too. From your mother last night."

Yermekov laughed brightly. "I have one word for you, Sabajan Hollant." She took a huge step forward, parried Saba's next blow, and seized Saba by the front of her shirt, dragging her in close. "Euhemenon."

Saba tore herself away, stumbling back. "What? What are you talking about?"

"Hah! See the great Sabajan Hollant entirely fail to feign ignorance," Yermekov declared. "Gather round, ladies and gents, see the great one crumble before your eyes!"

"By the boards and backdrops, I will bring *ruin* to your house."

"You'll have to, if you have any hope of winning against me," Yermekov purred. "I know all your secrets. Did you hear me? Euhemenon!"

Who'd told Yermekov about the play? It could only be Nazeya, that bitch. That traitor, that oathbreaker. Saba's over-energized adrenaline-fueled trembling calmed, then stilled.

Nazeya was the only one who could have told Yermekov, and who had any *reason* to do so. Saba cursed herself for a fool. How many times had she been betrayed by a beautiful woman? How many times had she given in to Idunet's seductive whispers in the back of her mind? Would she ever learn, or was she fated to squander every scrap of luck and fortune on a pretty face and a few flirtations?

To hell with the rules of formal combat. Those were for prissy nobles anyway. Saba hurled herself forward without warning and met Yermekov's blade with her own. She shoved it inelegantly aside and threw herself at Yermekov, catching her around the knees and heaving her onto the ground. Panting, Saba stood over her, rapier in hand, and rested the tip on that bitch's neck. "Yield?"

"Foul play!" Dauren screamed. "Stand down, Hollant!"

Saba spoke before Dauren's sword was half-drawn from its sheath. "Come another step closer and I'll pierce her through, see if I don't. Mind the horses."

"Technically, goading remarks are considered foul play as well," Talsyn said. "So your girl started it."

Saba turned her burning gaze back to Yermekov, pale and furious on the ground below her. "Zitka Yermekov, yield or die."

∽

Halfway back to town, Talsyn spoke up. "You gonna explain what's going on?"

"I made a mistake," Saba said. "Again."

"What was all that about Euhemenon?"

Saba swallowed hard. "Alvana and I found a lost Euhemenon play."

"A hoax. Probably a trick by the Reds."

"No. If they wanted to fake a Euhemenon play, they wouldn't have given the entire text of it to us first. But now the Reds know about it, so it's only a matter of time until..."

"Is it safe now?"

"I'm going to make it more safe."

Silence for a hundred yards. "How'd they find out? Who else knew, besides you and Alvana?"

"The translator," Saba said miserably. "It was written in Mangarha. I should have known better, but..."

"Who?"

"I'm going to go ahead and ask you not to punch me. Her name is Nazeya mes Akhal, and—"

"*Shit,*" Talsyn said. "Saba, you didn't."

"She was very convincing!"

"She's a Red!"

"How do you know that?"

Talsyn raised his eyes to the heavens. "*Saba.* You might not be good with names, but I am, and I'm not nearly so easily swayed by a pair of tits as you are."

"You're plenty swayed," Saba grumbled, petulant.

"She seduced you, didn't she."

"I haven't even kissed her."

"So she's playing it that way. Holding out until you give her everything she wants."

"Didn't seem like she was faking," Saba mumbled, her face hot with shame.

"Did she at any point say that she's such a big fan of yours? That you're her hero?"

Even Saba was aware of how conspicuous her silence was.

"She was playing you the whole time. Idunet's fucking *eyes,* Saba, this is why we stopped letting you go to bars by yourself." Saba gave him a sharp look. "What? You didn't think we were helping you get laid out of the goodness of our hearts, did you? For the last three years, you've only been allowed to be alone with women that one of us knew personally and could vouch for." He heaved a sigh. "We were all distracted after the Edict, but when you didn't walk face-first into a beehive shaped like a pair of tits, we thought, *Ah, perhaps Saba's days of sowing her wild oats are over. Perhaps she'll settle down and be a little more sensible."*

"Don't talk about me like I'm one of the boys," Saba snapped. "I don't think with my nethers."

"You *are* too trusting, though, and your vanity is second to none, so when some pretty girl comes simpering about how much she loves your work... You do see where I'm going with this, don't you?"

"I made a mistake," Saba said loudly. "I own that! I fucked up! But we haven't lost anything yet. We can fix this! So what if they know about the Euhemenon play? We know that they know! And they *don't* know that Alvana's nearly finished with a new one. We have an advantage! We can be ready for them."

"Ah," Talsyn said, airy. "What a nice change that will be."

The Reds paid up the fifty princes astonishingly quickly. The money was in Saba's hands by noon, and Alvana was freed just in time for the two of them to fly back to the theater so Saba could perform. Alvana sat backstage, hugging the Euhemenon play and her nearly-finished one and weeping softly, still grubby and bedraggled. Saba sent for Enryn, and when the day's business was done, he escorted Alvana home—her *and* the two plays.

Saba went straight back to her own rooms and was halfway through a large, miserable bottle of ale when the knock came on her door. She flung it open, took one look at who it was, and snarled, "You fucking bitch."

"Saba, please, let me in," Nazeya said desperately. "It wasn't me—"

She laughed. "Go to hell."

"Saba!" Nazeya caught the door as Saba tried to slam it. "I didn't do it. I swear, I didn't tell them. Yermekov was bragging about it—she still thinks she's won. She didn't care about the duel or the money. There's something else—"

"Why the fuck should I believe anything you say?"

"I *didn't tell them*, I can prove it—"

"Fuck your proof. You knew about the Euhemenon play, and you had reason to tell the Reds. You think you can convince me that one of the Lights is a spy? *They didn't even know about it.* You can go tell Yermekov that she can send me all the beautiful women she wants, but I won't be so easily beguiled."

"You're right, it wasn't your players." Nazeya pushed her way into the room; Saba was too incredulous to stop her. "Shut the door." Nazeya rummaged through her pockets. Her hands were shaking and her breath was short, as if she'd run all the way here. Mud splattered her hems. "Yermekov got a letter a couple days ago from our patron. She only started talking about the Euhemenon play after that." She drew a folded paper from her pocket and held it out.

Saba didn't take it immediately. She didn't even look at it. She stared hard at Nazeya, examining every tiny movement of her features. She was lying again, surely.

"Please," Nazeya whispered. "Just look at it."

Saba took it. The letter bore a broken wax seal, and when Saba tilted it towards the light—well. There was the Lord Seneschal's crest, impressed into the wax, clear and clean. It had even been rubbed with a little gold dust for contrast. Saba glanced up at Nazeya, who had crossed her arms and was watching her intently.

She unfolded the letter and read it.

"You see? It wasn't me," Nazeya said quietly. "I wouldn't tell. I *wouldn't*."

"Where did you get this?"

"I stole it. I knew as soon as Yermekov started crowing about Euhemenon that you'd think that I was the one who told her, and I *wasn't*. She got it from the Lord Seneschal—do you know who could have told him? Alvana's father is the owner of the book, isn't he?"

"What about your grandmother?" Saba asked sharply.

"She didn't, she swears it. You don't even have to believe me, I just..." She looked wretched. "You're in trouble and I wanted you to be on your guard."

Saba barely heard her. She was staring down at the letter. She said slowly, "There's only one other person with the information who could have gained anything by sharing it."

"Who?"

"My patron. The Lord Chancellor."

No one else had been in the room when she'd told the Lord Chancellor about the Euhemenon play. In this letter of Nazeya's, the Lord Seneschal wasn't bragging about finding out. He was annoyed. Incensed. He exhorted Yermekov to do something about it, promised to shield her from any legal ramifications. He sounded like a man who had been beaten at chess. "Your patron—he enjoys Euhemenon plays."

"Yes," Nazeya said, without hesitation. "Very much."

Yes, that was right—the Lord Chancellor had mentioned that, hadn't he? "Mine doesn't—or he didn't, I daresay, until he realized that he held a card in his hand that could sweep anything the Lord Seneschal played off the table. What do you think? He bragged? Used it to win some petty political fight? 'My troupe is working on something new, you know—a brand new, never before seen Euhemenon play...'" Saba turned away, seething.

"He was the only other one who knew?"

Saba looked at the letter again, now creased by the ferocity of her grip. "Men," she spat like a curse.

"Listen, Saba, please—Yermekov's going to try to steal it from you—"

"Oh my stars, do you think so?"

"*Listen* to me! They're going to Alvana's *tonight*. They were talking about taking *weapons*."

Saba's heart lurched so hard it sent a bolt of pain through her whole body. She scrambled for her shoes. "Why in the name of every god didn't you lead with that?"

"You would have thought I was trapping you," Nazeya said. "Why do you think Yermekov paid up so quickly on the wager? She knew the play would be hidden or protected, she knew you wanted bail money to get Alvana out—and that *Alvana would know where it was.*"

"Out of my way," Saba said, seizing her coat. She dove out the door, down the stairs, and into the night, heedless of whether Nazeya was following.

~

Saba stopped just in front of Alvana's door, almost too scared to open it and discover... whatever was inside. With a gulp, she tapped. "Alvana?"

She heard a whimper in reply and, weak with relief, flung the door open. Alvana sat in the middle of the floor, wreckage scattered all around—papers and books strewn in drifts across the floor, clothing ripped from the wardrobe. Saba was on her knees by Alvana's side in a heartbeat, wrapping her up in her arms and squeezing tight. "Sweetheart, sweetheart. Did they hurt you?"

"They took the plays, Saba," Alvana said, her voice thick.

Saba pulled back and ran her hands over Alvana's shoulders, pushing the hair back out of her face—she had the beginnings of a black eye and a split lip. Saba's heart froze solid. She touched Alvana's face with her fingertips. She hadn't cried yet, Saba could tell.

"They had knives, and—well, I knew they were prop knives, so I wasn't that scared. I told them I wouldn't give it up, and they did all this." Alvana gestured around at the room. "I tried to hit Dauren. She hit me back. Zitka found the plays on her own, behind the loose brick."

"Fuck." Saba said quietly. "This is too far. This is the last straw. They can take the plays, they can ruin us all they like, but they *don't. Hurt. You.*"

"They don't care about sneaking anymore. I don't understand why. Last time..."

"Last time, they had an elaborate scheme, yeah."

"I don't even know how they found out."

"It was their patron." Saba shifted to sit beside her. "And he got it from ours. I expect they were measuring their dicks or whatever ridiculous posturing those two get up to, and ours thought he'd score an easy blow."

"Oh," said Alvana. "Wait, how do you know that?"

Saba released a long breath. "I saw a letter the Lord Seneschal sent Yermekov."

"How?" Alvana pulled away, staring at her. "You—you didn't *break into Yermekov's flat?*"

"Does it look like I have Handsome with me?" Saba asked sharply. "I would have brought him too, if I'd done that. The translator I found was Nazeya mes Akhal. She's the one who discovered the play in the first place. She knew I'd think she was the snitch, so she brought me the letter to prove her innocence."

"Nazeya who?"

"Oh, one of the Reds," Saba said, valiantly attempting a casual tone.

"Saba!"

"I know, I know! But she's had fifty chances to fuck me over and she hasn't."

Alvana put her face in her hands. "Saba, why didn't you tell me?"

"I just wanted to get us some raw material to work with!

That book wasn't supposed to have a fucking *lost Euhemenon play* in it."

"Lost and found and lost again," Alvana said, muffled in her palms. "Saba, what are we going to do?"

Saba glared across the room for a long moment, then turned and kissed Alvana's forehead. "I'll take care of it."

"Saba," Alvana said, her voice breaking as Saba scrambled to her feet. "Saba, where are you going? Tell me!"

"I shan't, and don't ask me to."

"You're going to get yourself arrested, aren't you?"

Saba made herself smile at Alvana and turned to the door.

"Don't go alone," Alvana said urgently. "Promise! If the Reds catch you, they'll snap you in half. Don't go alone."

Saba thought for a moment, then nodded. "Promise."

The Theater of Truth was sleepy and nearly empty when she arrived. Its fires were burning low, the patrons had settled into exhausted, drunken half-stupors, and Enryn was cleaning glasses.

Saba strode up to the bar, leaned across it, and seized Enryn's arms. "By our friendship, by the boards and backdrops, by the Lord of Song's silver name: If you love me true, you'll come with me *now*."

Without a blink, without a heartbeat's hesitation, Enryn set down the glass, tossed the cloth on the counter and called over to the barkeep: "Family emergency. Leaving early." He vaulted over the bar with an astounding grace for a man of his size. Saba had never loved him more. "What's happening?"

"Reds."

"Shit. Bad?"

"They hurt Alvana and they have the new plays."

"Plays? Plural?"

"Yes."

"Alvana's?"

"One of them is."

"Shit." They reached the doors and rushed out into the night. "What do you want to do?"

"I don't know. We have to—stop them. Somehow. Please, I need you. I know I have no right to ask."

Enryn took her by the shoulders and steered her into an alley, away from anyone who might see or overhear them. "You have the right. Do we know where they took the plays? Do we even know where the Reds are right now?"

"No."

"Okay. Breathe. I'll tell you what we should do," Enryn said. "And then I'll tell you what we're going to do. We *should* run straight to the Lord Chancellor and tell him what happened."

Saba groaned and threw her hands in the air. "He won't *do* anything! He's useless! He won't listen!"

"I know."

"He doesn't know how things work on the street! The Reds are probably already copying out Euhemenon and rehearsing it as we speak—*they're* not idiots! We don't have time to argue with our patron about it, and he'll say that it's *our* fault somehow!"

"I know. Which is why we're not going to do that."

Saba looked at him helplessly. "Then *what?*"

He rested his hand on her shoulder. "You're a woman of honor, Sabajan Hollant." he said. "You've been playing a different game than the Reds have been playing."

"Don't I fucking know it."

"They won't play your game. If you want to win this, you have to play theirs." He nodded solemnly. "So let's go set the Red Theater on fire."

"Talesyn's tits and testicles, are you insane—"

"They can copy and rehearse all the plays they want. They can't perform them without a theater."

Saba spluttered. "There's a hundred theaters in the city! They'll find another one!"

"Mmm, they won't. How many troupes are *we* on good terms with? Good enough terms to swan up to them and say, 'Hey, can we borrow your theater? Ours burned down'?"

Saba winced. "One or two. And they'd extort us for it. Outright highway robbery."

"Exactly," he said. "The Reds have even fewer allies than we do. Yermekov and Dauren haven't exactly stayed loyal to their roots. They don't have anyone to ask for favors. So let's go burn down their theater."

Saba felt herself slipping towards agreement and scrabbled desperately at the cliff of reason, clinging to the edge by her fingertips. "This is madness. This is— "

"They've had too much time to set up their plans—go for the throat or lose this hand of cards and the whole game. Let's *end this. Tonight.* What have we to lose? Tell me that. They backed us into a corner—if we lose *two* plays, the Lord Chancellor will withdraw his patronage and we'll be humiliated by the Reds again. If we burn down their theater, he'll withdraw and, in the worst case scenario, we go to prison. Either way, we've *already lost.*"

"So we might as well take those bitches down with us," Saba said slowly, a cold and terrible calm settling over her. "Either we lose, or we all lose. Yes. All right. Let's go."

~

They spoke no more until they came to Lammerel Square, dominated by the Red Theater looming huge on one side. It was dark and quiet, the shops all locked up, the residences above still and slumbering. "We should go inside first," Saba said. "Look around. See what valuables *they've* left lying around."

"You sure? It's a risk."

"Yes, come on."

In most of Avaris (and certainly in Brassing-on-Abona, its capital) theaters had the same rough layout—at least the front of the house did, the parts seen by the public: The ostentatious front entrance, the circular central yard, the galleries ringing it.

It was the back of the house which would vary. There was no norm to adhere to there—every theater backstage Saba had ever stuck her nose into was a rabbit warren of storage rooms. If any treasure was to be found, that's where she'd find it.

Saba and Enryn didn't do anything so suspicious as *creep*, but they stuck to the deepest shadows and felt their way along the side of the theater until Saba's fingers brushed across the wood of the rear door. Locked, of course, but there was a small sloped roof above the door to keep the rain off the threshold, and above that, a window.

It was effortless for Enryn to boost her up so she could scramble onto the little roof. When she pushed against the mullioned windowpanes—nope. Locked too. She snorted at herself. What had she been thinking, anyway? Had she really thought she could so easily find a conveniently unlatched window, right within reach?

Well, the theater was going to burn anyway. What did it matter if there were damages to it before that?

"Give me your coat," she whispered to Enryn. When he handed it up, Saba draped it over her head, wrapped her fist in one enormous sleeve, and smashed the window.

It was loud, but not nearly as loud as she'd feared it would be, though the sound of the shower of glass rattling off the cobblestones was unfortunate. She was still for a moment, straining to hear for cries of alarm. In the silence, she tossed

Enryn's coat back down to him, hauled herself up to the sill, unlatched the window, and opened it—better to avoid slicing herself to ribbons on any of the jagged leftover glass still clinging to the windowframe.

Once, years and years ago, back before they'd had patrons or had lost all their boys to the Edict, before Saba and Alvana had ever started their own troupe, Saba had poked her nose into the backstage of the Red Theater. It had been new-built in those days, still smelling of fresh wood and thatch, still bright with garish paint—which had not so much faded as it had *mellowed* into something more distinguished than the scarlet it had been in its youth. In those days, there had been a management office on the ground floor, quite near the rear door. That seemed as good a place as any to stash valuables.

Saba found the stairs by nearly falling headfirst down them and cursed herself. "Saw my life flash before my eyes there," she muttered. She continued slowly, feeling with her feet for each step, her legs shaking with adrenaline from the near-fall. "Hey there, Nevainyë," she crooned under her breath as she descended. "Don't talk to *you* much at all, do I? Remember me? Saba? I'm more pals with your brother Talesyn these days, but I used to sing to you when I was scared of the dark as a kid, remember that? Be nice and I'll make Alvana write a real good play about you, all right?"

Maybe appealing to the Queen of Shadows worked, because it was slightly easier to navigate through the ground floor level—the curtains between the stage and the backstage had been drawn aside, and there was just enough ambient light from the moons to show her the vague shapes of things in her path.

The management office was unlocked—and still an office, Saba knew immediately. Nowhere else would smell so much like old copies of plays written out by hand with oak-gall ink, or fresh ones printed on the new presses. Inside, she identified a large desk by feel, and after trying a couple of the drawers, she discovered a packet of matches. "The gods help those who help themselves," she murmured. When she struck the match, she found, to her pleasure, that there was an oil lamp right beside her. "Well, well, well, Clevertongue—or should I say Lord of Flame? Don't hear that one quite so much, eh? I gotta say, I am *feeling* you with me tonight, O pyrolatric prince. Cinereous sovereign. Incendiary imperator."

Her deity appropriately flattered and the wick of the lamp lit, Saba rifled through the drawers of the desk—there were bills of sale, records and accounts, ledgers, all useless for her purposes. There were several copies of old plays—also useless.

In the end, all she found of worth was a handful of spare coins in the back of one drawer, about a quarter of a prince in total. Distantly, she heard the tolling bell at the temple marking the fourth hour of the night, and cursed. How long had she been in here? Enryn would be wetting himself with anxiety.

"Fuck. Here I go," she muttered, and hurled the oil lamp at the wall.

It shattered quite magnificently; the flame licked up to the rafters and down onto the desk, the scattered papers. She watched the fire for only a handful of seconds; it was already spreading and catching at an alarming rate.

She wondered, belatedly, whether Lord Talesyn was the sort to take offense. On one hand: Fire, which was his. On the other hand: A theater, also his. She cleared her throat and muttered, "Don't be mad at me, Silverthroat, you know we're buddies. Idunet made me do it."

Theological quibble resolved, she fled.

Getting out of the theater was easier; she only had to unlock the back door and walk out. Enryn nearly jumped out of his skin before he saw it was her. "There's watchmen," he whispered urgently. "We have to leave—there's one who'll *definitely* recognize me if he sees me up cloase."

"What? How?"

"He's a *fan* of mine," Enryn hissed, bundling her along. "Some people are fans of the theater, *Sabajan Hollant.* Forget the plan. If we burn the Red and they catch us—what's that face for? What?"

"Uh," Saba said. "I already set the fire."

"Shit." He grabbed her arm and they flew down the nearest alley.

"Quieter!" she hissed.

Enryn's big lug feet were slapping against the cobblestones, echoing off the sides of the buildings. "No time," he panted. "The Lady of Hours is feeling merciless."

Voices behind them, footsteps, a shout of alarm. The dreaded cry: "Oi! Halt!" And then, moments later: "Fire! *Fire!*"

"Fuck," Saba said. "Split up—meet you back at the Truth."

The watch caught up with her three streets later.

The next morning, Saba languished in her jail cell and contemplated her fate. She was mulling over the likelihood of execution versus exile when she heard distressed voices down the hall. A moment later, she recognized them and sat up sharply on her bench. The others—the Lights. Her troupe.

The warden unlocked the door and flung in Artagne, Inneo, and Mabeth, all grimy with sweat and dirt, all three of them with sawdust in their hair, and all three of them clutching bloodied cloths to their arms or sides.

"What the fuck happened?" Saba cried.

"The Reds happened," Inneo said darkly. "They came

with swords. Revenge for their theater, they said. There was a fight."

"Gods," Saba breathed. "Are you all right? All of you?"

"Nothing life-threatening," Artagne said.

"The others?" Saba asked, terrified to hear the answer.

"Tal's being patched up by the healers. He took a bad blow to the head. And Katre... Don't know if she'll make it. Gut wound."

Saba put her head in her hands. "Fuck. Fuck."

"You want to tell us your side of the story?" Inneo snapped. "You want to tell us why you had a whimsy for a bit of arson?"

"They hurt Alvana. They stole the plays." Saba swallowed hard. "I had to do something. I got Enryn and we went together."

Mabeth slid down the opposite wall to the floor. "That's it, isn't it. It's over."

"Without a doubt," said Inneo. "At least, the Lights are over and Sabajan Hollant is over."

"Maybe I should just go back to Vinte," Artagne muttered. "Leave, like Maddie did. None of us are working in this city again."

"I didn't have a choice," Saba snapped. "They had our long-lost *Euhemenon* play—surprise! We had one! We were going to be immortalized for that alone! But they took it, and Alvana's new one. A new one, do you hear?"

The other three were silent. Artagne leaned against the wall and looked out the barred window. Inneo sat on the bench and stared at the ground.

"If you're so sure that I fucked up," Saba said, "tell me what I should have done instead. What would have happened if the Reds had performed those plays? We don't have the money to keep going like this for much longer."

"How long would we have had, if you'd left them alone?" Artagne asked. "How long do you think?"

"Honestly? A couple months. We needed Alvana's play. We *desperately* needed that Euhemenon play. If they'd left us even one, we could have scraped by."

Artagne pursed her lips and gazed at Saba for a long time. "All right."

Inneo's head snapped up. "All right? *All right*? You forgive her?"

"No," Artagne whispered, turning again to the window. "But I understand her."

Inneo spluttered.

"Are you unconvinced?" Artagne asked. "Answer her: What would you have done differently?"

"We could have talked to them," Mabeth said quietly. "We could have negotiated *something*, couldn't we?"

"Fat chance," Inneo snarled.

"But we used to be friends."

Artagne and Saba said, in unison, "Well now, hold on—"

"I wouldn't say *friends*," Saba said.

"Let's not exaggerate," said Artagne.

"Friendly rivals," Mabeth amended. "We used to talk to them. We used to go to their plays, and they used to come to ours. We used to meet them in the Theater of Truth and bicker with them—trading barbs in public was practically the second half of the day's performance. Alvana and Yermekov were together for a little while, and Katre was sleeping with Jenny Peyford for a few months—"

"She *what*!" Saba squawked. "*When?*"

"And before they left, Felix Foxbridge and Marta Ngotho were both trying to court Artagne—"

"*Succeeding* at courting Artagne," said Artagne.

"The point is, there was competition, but it wasn't *stupid*. They were reasonable, rational people once upon a time. They still are. People don't change like that, only circumstances change."

Saba huffed a humorless laugh. "Oh, how I'd love to sit down with Yermekov and shout at each other until we've drafted an armistice. If only we'd been that smart three years ago."

"At least the Reds are as stupid as you are," Inneo muttered. "They attacked us—that won't go unpunished. Lord Chancellor may dearly wish to wash his hands of us, but the Lord Seneschal's Women storming his troupe's theater? That's an opportunity for political gain that he won't discard so easily."

Saba sat up straight. "Oh," she breathed. "They got arrested too, then! Hah!"

"That is a silver lining," Artagne allowed. "A very thin one."

Inneo snorted. "I wish you'd been there to see it when they came in, Saba. It was a *sight*."

"Twelve of them ran into the theater while we were rehearsing," said Mabeth, with a faint wry smile. "Naked swords in their hands, hair flying every which way, and I stood there gaping like a fish and thought—" A half-laugh bubbled up through her voice, "I thought, 'Huh, this is just like the assassination scene in *Caelavius*!'"

"Oh, so did I!" said Inneo.

"Where did they get the swords?" Saba asked. "I burned their theater down—they wouldn't have had props."

"It was mostly knives," Artagne said. "Knives and daggers. Yermekov had a messer, though, a proper one."

"Not that she knew how to use it," Inneo said.

"Was..." Saba hardly dared to ask. "Was Nazeya there?"

"Nazeya mes Akhal? No." Artagne narrowed her eyes. "Wait, what do you care about her?"

"Nothing," Saba said, too quickly. All three of them fixed

her with sharp, knowing expressions; she groaned. "No, no, don't say anything. That was bad acting on my part."

"What *do* you care about Nazeya mes Akhal?" Inneo said.

"She's... you know. A good player."

"And a Red," Inneo said, incredulous. "It's been years since you admitted the Reds were good."

"The Reds aren't good," Saba said firmly. "They're hacks. But Nazeya..."

Mabeth, Inneo, and Artagne exchanged glances. "Saba," Mabeth said delicately. "Are you sleeping with her?"

"Absolutely not!"

"You'd like to be sleeping with her, I bet," said Inneo.

"Hey now, listen. Let's keep things fair, okay—"

"Nazeya mes Akhal is very beautiful," Artagne said. "And Saba thinks she's a good player. Of course she wants to sleep with her."

"And? I'm allowed to want stupid things, aren't I?"

"She's the one who came backstage as your *visitor* few weeks ago," Artagne continued. "The one you so quickly dragged away from the dressing room. I didn't figure out why her face was so familiar until a few days later, but I recalled how swiftly and mercilessly you threw her out, and I chose not to follow up on it."

"She's not a spy! She's *not.*"

"She's definitely a spy." Artagne sighed. "That explains our terrible luck the past few months."

"I swear by the boards and backdrops and Songspinner's lute-strings, she's not a spy. Or—well, if anything, she's a spy for *me*, not for them."

They got the rest of it out of her in bits and pieces: the book, the translation, the play. Five hours later, they had talked themselves hoarse and come to no conclusions.

They were all scattered around the cell, sitting in dour silence, when the warden's key scraped and creaked in the lock and the door swung open. "Out you come," he said flatly.

"Out?" Saba shot to her feet. "What for? Are we being released?"

"Which if you is Hollant? Someone's here to talk to you."

Saba grasped Inneo's arm, breathless with hope. "The Lord Chancellor?"

"Nah," the warden said. "A woman."

He led her down the hall to another room where, sitting on a rough wooden bench at a table as if she were a queen and it was her throne... was Iracena. She was wearing *eyewateringly* fine clothing—deep green brocade with perfectly white lace cuffs, a latticework partlet across her shoulders made of velvet ribbon with a pearl or square-cut green tourmaline at each intersection, her chestnut hair caught up in a matching net. Pearl and tourmaline earrings, too.

Saba glanced between her and the guard. "This is it?" she asked the guard, who shrugged. "You're it?" she asked Iracena.

"Watch your mouth," Iracena snapped—her badly-faked snobby accent was suddenly *much* improved. "I might be about to do you a favor."

Saba stared at her. "What in the world for?"

Iracena gestured to the guard. "Bring her a chair."

Saba had been wondering idly in the back of her mind where the fuck the Reds had found a costumier who could do work like *that* (or possibly how Iracena had managed to get snapped up as some rich fuck's mistress so quick), but as the guard sprang to obey without hesitation, she jolted in epiphany: Iracena's shitty accent wasn't badly-faked snob, it was badly-faked *commoner*. Huh.

"You're in an unfortunate situation," Iracena said, when Saba was seated. "Mere exile will be getting off lightly. I've come to offer you another opportunity."

Saba was barely listening. "*Is* du Cassa your real name?"

"No. As I was saying—"

"If you wanted to be a player so bad, why hide that you're... Oh. Because they'll all think you bought your way into the troupe, right?"

Iracena flushed with anger. "Are you even *listening*?"

"I was looking at your thingy," Saba gestured to her own chest. "On your tits. Partlet thingy. It's nice."

Iracena stared at her, outraged. "Madam Hollant, it may *benefit you* to pay attention to what I am offering." Ugh. Iracena. Just the worst. "I will post bail for the troupe. In exchange, you'll cast me in your plays."

"Your pick of which part, I suppose?"

"That's only fair."

"Reds didn't treat you right, eh?"

Iracena pursed her lips. "They kept giving me *bit parts*."

"And? You're new. Everyone does it that way."

"I don't want to do it that way," she snapped. "I'm good. I'm as good as anyone."

Saba found herself distracted by the tourmalines twinkling from Iracena's ears. "What *is* your real name, anyway?"

Iracena tapped her fingernails on the table slowly, one by one. "Iracena Shereham. I'm Earl Highwich's daughter." After a moment, she added, "I thought you'd recognized me, actually."

"Did you? Why?"

"That comment you made."

"I make a lot of comments."

"The one about whether I grew up thinking of the Master of Revels as an uncle or if I was childhood friends with the Lord Seneschal's daughter. Yes, on both counts."

Saba failed to entirely stifle a smirk. "Lucky coincidence."

"I figured that out when you didn't stop humiliating me."

"Oh, *please*. Look, Iracena. Or Honorable Lady Shereham, whatever I'm supposed to call you."

"Lady Shereham," she said briskly. "'Honorable' is for viscounts' and barons' children."

"Sure, whatever. If you want speaking parts in the plays, if you want to have retroactively earned them, you're going to have to take direction. There's debate, in circles of idiots, about whether the Lights or the Reds are the finest troupe in the city; there's even debate about the best playwright in the city, though clearly the answer is Alvana. But there's *no* debate about the best director in the city. It's me. You want speaking parts in exchange for getting us out of this one specific mess?" Saba took a deep breath. "Fine. I'll give you speaking parts in as many of our plays as you want, for one year. But you have to agree that you'll trust me to do my job properly."

"I won't be *humiliated.*"

"If you're moving like a constipated chicken, I'm going to tell you that, *in those words*, so that you can stop. You want to look beautiful, don't you? You want the audience to admire you. You want everyone to know how good you are." Iracena's eyes flickered. "Guess what, chickadee? I want that for you too. If you're in one of my plays and the whole audience is wildly in love with you, that *benefits* me, do you understand? If they're all talking about how you're the best romantic heroine anyone's ever seen—Artagne who?—then I'll be *dancing* to the Theater of Truth that night." Saba paused long enough for Iracena to jump in and say something, but she remained silent, her eyes filled with fire. "I would never humiliate you on stage. But I'm going to scold you in rehearsal, just like I scold everyone else."

"Not like everyone else. You have favorites."

"No, actually, I don't. I have friends, I have colleagues, I have business partners. But if Artagne or Tal moves like a constipated chicken, I'm going to tell them so too, and I'll do it right in front of everyone. The reason you don't see me shouting at them quite as often is just that they have more practice than you do. They know what they're doing. And, by the way, the plays that you were rehearsing with us? We've played them all before, other than *Some by Virtue Fall*. The shareholders know those plays back to front and sideways—all the shouting about them happened years ago." Saba heaved a theatrical sigh. "If only you'd gotten to see us properly rehearsing a *new* play. But those are my terms—you take direction like everyone else, and after one year, you go back to earning your parts just like everyone else."

"Fine."

"Do we need to have a lawyer write this up for us, or are you the sort of gentlewoman who abides by a code of honor?" Saba offered her hand for Iracena to shake. She did, slowly.

"I have the honor for a verbal agreement if you do."

"Great. Now," Saba turned to the warden at the door. "She's bailing me and all my friends out. Do I need to go back to my cell or shall I just stay here?"

Iracena got to her feet. "Stay here," she said.

"One more question—you really didn't like working for the Reds?"

Iracena shrugged. "What can I say? You're a better director than Yermekov and Dauren are."

The Theater of Lights was, thankfully, unburnt—the Reds evidently hadn't posted bail themselves yet. The front door was closed but not locked, which gave Saba a moment of terror. Anyone could have wandered in and ransacked it, but all the troupe found was an elderly woman, who was sitting in the twopenny gallery with her two pennies clutched in her hand and already cranky that the day's performance was late—and then *outraged* when informed that it was canceled entirely.

Saba let the others deal with her and took Alvana into the dressing room. "Poor dear," she crooned. "It's been a terrible ordeal, hasn't it? Jailed *twice!* Let's get you a bath and fresh clothes."

"There's no point, Saba," Alvana said, utterly defeated. "It's all over."

"Not yet," Saba said, making her voice bright. "We've got a theater and a troupe. We can do anything. Now stay here and I'll get you a bucket."

When she returned, Alvana was sitting and moping in the middle of the dressing room floor in her undergarments.

"Chin up." Saba thunked the bucket in front of her. "I think there's soap around here somewhere, isn't there?"

"There's no point. The money, Saba."

"We've managed before and we'll manage now," she said, rummaging in the drawers of the cabinet for the soap.

"And what if we can't?"

"Then we'll close down in a month and do something else. *You* don't have to worry. Any troupe in the city would wet themselves for the chance at a Stillgrail play. All you have to do is keep writing."

"But I don't want to write for anyone but you."

"Then when we get exiled for arson and breaking-and-entering, we'll go abroad and find some other troupe to take us in. Pretty good for me, eh? I'm the one who gets to say that I come with a genius friend and that we're a package deal." Saba found the tin of soft soap and dropped it in Alvana's lap.

"Don't be silly," Alvana sniffled. "Anyone would take you."

"Debatable. I've made more enemies than you have. A lot of people would like to see me cast down." She shrugged. "I'm a director because I'm bad at taking direction. Nobody wants a player who's so full of themselves that they won't listen to anybody else." Alvana snorted and shot Saba a *look*. Saba grinned. "I know my flaws, sweetheart."

"That's not what I was thinking," Alvana said, slowly rubbing the soap to a froth.

"Oh?"

"You'll be mad."

"Say it."

"Iracena."

"What about her?"

Alvana gave her another look. "You're just the same, you two."

"Now see here!"

"Like a pair of angry spoons."

"Alvana!"

"Told you you'd be mad. It's true, though."

"It's not!"

"She doesn't take direction well and she doesn't listen to anybody else. Remember when you were sixteen? The Wicket Street Players? You only lasted a month. Everyone was surprised that Fatter Alfred tolerated you that long."

Saba couldn't actually argue with that. She'd been surprised herself. "What's your point, woman?"

Alvana shrugged. "Do you want to be friends with her?"

"Oh, for fuck's sake."

"You're stuck with her for a year."

Saba narrowed her eyes. "You think I should *take her under my wing* or some shit."

Alvana primly continued scrubbing.

"I'm not going to take her under my wing."

"She's just like you."

"She's nothing like me."

"She'd be a good director."

Saba made a scathing noise.

"How many people tolerated you when you were young

and angry and stupid? Dozens. Because they all knew you were something special. Iracena knows what she wants, she doesn't like listening to anyone else, and she has a vision as clear as crystal. Just needs to learn technique, that's all."

Saba grumbled. "She comes from rich folk."

"Play nice with her and she might contribute a little—buy us a play here and there, pay the tab at the Truth..."

"If she starts paying for things, she'll end up a *patron*. And then we'll be dealing with her *forever.*"

"But we could buy new plays." Alvana turned wistful. "If we could get our shit together, we could hire Enryn as a back-of-the-house man."

Somehow, *he* hadn't gotten arrested last night—Saba was still baffled. "He told me he'd learn to sew if we wanted him to."

"With those huge hands?"

"We'll just get him a really big needle, don't worry about it."

Alvana snorted and rinsed the cloth in the water. "First, plays."

"Do you think they'll try to sell the Euhemenon play? Bargain with it in exchange for theater space?"

"If they can convince anyone else it's real. So long as your translator keeps quiet, they'll have to either admit they stole it or say that they have no provenance for it."

"Will anyone care about that? Fatter Alfred used to tell stories about the year after Oswyn Blackthumb died—everyone and their mum was finding previously-unknown plays of hers in their attics, though mysteriously none of them were in her actual handwriting."

"We could be the ones to bargain with them, you know. Give them some of our performance days in exchange for—no, we can't afford that, can we?"

Saba shook her head.

Alvana's lower lip wobbled for a moment, but she clenched her jaw suddenly, seized the bucket, and upended it over her head.

"Uh," said Artagne, pausing in the doorway. "Am I interrupting?"

"Not at all. Could you get Alvana some clean clothes?"

"Of course. But I just came to ask... What play are we doing tomorrow?"

"Can't be anything too physical, what with how you people are all injured."

"Let's do *Some by Virtue Fall*," Alvana said, wiping the sodden hair and streams of water off her face. "Why not, right?"

"Oh," said Saba. "Oh, *yes*. Why not, indeed! We're already teetering on the brink; it's no particular extra risk at this point. Do we—Lord of Song, we still have those five scripts! Artagne, clothes for Alvana! And get the others!"

"That'll be nice. Blaze of glory," Alvana said wetly as Artagne flew from the room. "We'll have to shuffle the roles."

"Leave it to me."

≈

"We have *days* before we're summoned to court," Saba said, standing in the yard with the troupe arrayed on the stage before her. "The fastest we've ever learned and staged a play was five days. We're going to beat that, because I'm definitely going to be sentenced guilty unless the Lord Chancellor comes through for us—unlikely. But enough of that. Iracena, if I might borrow you while the others get warmed up." Frowning, Iracena descended; Saba led her to one of the galleries and sat with her on the frontmost bench. "So. What's the goal?"

"What?"

"The goal. For this play. What's the goal?"

'I'm going to play the—"

'No, our goal. Our *collective* goal."

Iracena blinked at her. "To save you and the others from being convic—"

'No. That's up to lawyers and courts. Try again."

'I don't bloody know. You want to put on something good enough to—"

'Stop. You got it. Right there. We just want to put on a good play. Ideally, a *great* play. One that people will tell their grandchildren about. Are you on board?"

'Yes, obviously," Iracena scoffed. "What do you take me for?"

'Great." Saba ignored the rest of that. "You know the play already. You were in it. So let's cast it, you and me."

That surprised her. The sour, haughty expression she always seemed to wear cracked and vanished. 'I beg your pardon?"

'Start with you. You want a good part. But you want to pick the best part for *you*, not the best part in the play. Right?"

'Wrong."

'And if the best part, the star of the show, is a comedic knight? Low comedy, that is—do you want to fart and swear and drunkenly carouse across the stage? Or do you want the counter-part, the one that has some dignity?"

Iracena settled back into mulishness. 'Point taken."

'That's the first lesson, girl. You don't take the best part, nor the one with the most lines. You take the part that's best for you. Which one is that, in this play?"

After a long, wary silence, Iracena said, "The queen."

Surprising—or perhaps entirely unsurprising. The queen had significantly fewer lines than Aucien and Cosima, but she had a quiet power, and she had *influence*. Saba found herself happy to give Iracena that part. 'All right, I think you'll do a fine job with that. How about everyone else? Do the whole cast."

Iracena stared at her.

Saba shrugged. "I might not take all your suggestions, but I want you to argue each part for each person. You know them and their capabilities well enough."

"All right," Iracena said slowly, as if waiting for the punch-line of some mean prank. "Artagne for Cosima."

"Yep, easy. There's no one like Artagne for romantic heroines."

"Mabeth for her lady-in-waiting."

Saba tilted her head and considered. "A possibility. Why?"

"She looks sneaky. The lady-in-waiting sneaks."

"Hm. Not good enough, but we'll come back to it. What about the men's roles?"

"Inneo for Aucien."

Saba shook her head immediately. "Inneo hates playing a simpering hero. She'll do it, but she'd be better elsewhere."

"Fine. You play him, then."

"No."

Iracena threw her hands in the air. "Are you going to shoot down every suggestion I make?"

"I take supporting roles, because I'm the director and I'm busy telling everyone else where to stand. I'm playing the Lord of Temptation—he only appears twice."

"And you're *fine* with that?"

"I am. It doesn't matter how many lines you have, it matters what you *do* with them. If you're good enough, you can steal the show with one monologue in one scene. Or less. Did you ever see Pinch Cooper playing Quinceflower in *The Forest Queen's Wedding*?"

"No."

"They were one of the best bit actors in the city. Pinch could come on stage for the space of ten heartbeats, crack one joke, and steal the entire show. That's what I do—I take smaller roles I can have fun with for a scene or two, and I let people like Artagne sparkle through the whole play. For Aucien, then, we'll have Tal—"

Just beside them, the front door creaked open. Saba looked up and jumped to her feet.

Zitka Yermekov stood on the threshold, hands raised. "I come in peace. Probably."

"Get the fuck out! How dare you!" Saba filled her lungs and projected loud enough to rattle the windowpanes across the street: "Everyone to the yard! Bring me a sword!"

"I just want to talk. Truly."

"You think you can walk in here and sit down for a *chat*?"

"I think that if you'd like to save your own skins, you'll give me twenty minutes of your time," Yermekov said softly.

"I don't fucking trust you an inch," Saba hissed.

"We both made mistakes. Things got out of hand, and now there are consequences. Talk to me." Yermekov hadn't come a step further inside, still showing her palms. "Please," she said, even softer. "You and I are each other's only chance to get out of this alive. Us *and* our troupes."

Saba looked around the theater—all the others had rushed to the yard and were standing in frozen silence, tense as drawn crossbows and ready to act at her slightest command. "We talk here. In my territory. None of this fucking neutral ground bullshit. You came to me? We sit *here*."

"Acceptable."

"You care about the others listening in?"

"Not at all, but I want to speak to *you*. I want a chance to convince *you*."

Saba turned to the yard and stomped down the steps. "I want all of you in the galleries, and I want you to watch her close." She swept her arm around, pointing in a wide circle. "Someone watching from every angle. If she tries anything sneaky, shout." As the others moved into place, Saba sat down in the middle of the yard, right on the sawdust, and gestured Yermekov to a spot opposite her. Yermekov obeyed without any fuss.

"First, an apology," Yermekov said. "I've done things to you that weren't right. I have no excuse." She closed her eyes. "These patrons, Hollant. What a mistake."

"You're telling me," Saba said dryly.

"Patronage has influenced me in ways that I don't like. It's warped me into a person that I barely recognize. I've made choices purely to please and flatter my patron, choices that went against my honor and my character. I trampled on you to grasp at what breadcrumbs he threw for us. It was wrong of me, and I wish I hadn't done it, and I'm sorry."

"I don't believe you yet."

"I don't blame you. We are both women of prudence and good sense—most of the time. Well. Some of the time."

"Some of the time," Saba agreed.

"In our attempts at prudence, we were dragged into a war that was not of our choosing. Our patrons used us as pawns, and now that we've hit each other as hard as we both could, they've dropped us. We've..." She let her breath hiss out through her teeth. "We've outlived our usefulness."

Saba blinked. "Your patron dropped you?"

"This morning. Nazeya brought us the news. It was her idea that I should speak to you." Yermekov gave a wry half-smile. "She was to be my Artagne Grey within two years." Her eyes flicked up to glance at Artagne, looming on the stage directly behind Saba. "But that won't happen now unless we can help each other."

"Help each other, hah! I've heard that in plays before, right before someone gets stabbed in the back."

"You're on the line for arson; Alvana, for breaking and entering. You're under financial strain. Your troupe will splinter within six months, if not sooner. Blink if I'm right," she said, right as Saba blinked. Shit. "On our side, nearly all of us are charged with public duelling and attempted murder— not to mention, we've found ourselves without a theater. There are four possible outcomes.

"First option: We both distrust each other. I go to jail, my players go to jail, you go to jail, Alvana goes to jail. The few remaining Reds and Lights close up shop. We are all forgotten.

"Second option: I trust you, but you betray me. The Reds are eliminated. You totter along for another half-year, and then you too die out.

"Third option: You trust me, but I betray you. The Lights are eliminated—probably you'd sell your theater to pay for your court fees, but you'd rather burn this one down too before you sold it to *us*. So we Reds wander the streets for a bit, briefly become a traveling troupe, and likely disband by year's end.

"Fourth option: We work together. We save each other in the short term, no one goes to jail, and then..." Yermekov folded her hands in her lap. "And then we have more conversations, as equals, about how to survive. This option is the *only way* we get out with our lives and careers intact. There is no other choice—we both win, or neither of us does."

Saba looked around. Her troupe—her *friends*—stood at the railings of the galleries all around her, watching.

"It *is* stupid, isn't it," she said. "The feud. The *war*. Being thrown at each other like we're troops instead of troupes."

"Men are stupid," Yermekov said. "Noble men, doubly so."

"It did get out of hand."

"Yes." They were silent, and then Yermekov spoke again: "They say you can't undo what's been done, but I disagree. Tapestries can be unwoven; injuries can be healed. A broken chair can be mended—not *unbroken*, but mended. I ask you,

Sabajan Hollant, what's the most important thing? What's your goal?"

Hadn't Saba just lectured Iracena about this half an hour ago? She could not bring herself to dissemble. Not now, not about a question that important. "Show them a good play. The best play anyone has ever seen, even the Lord of Players himself."

"Hence our rivalry—we share the same goal. Sabajan, we've fucked each other over enough times that we'll probably never like each other. Nevertheless, I'm asking you to trust me just enough to save our necks."

She extended her hand. Saba looked at it for a long time, looked around the galleries again at all her players watching, waiting.

"All right," Saba said, and took Yermekov's hand.

$$\sim$$

The courtroom was packed full. The Lights clustered together on one side of the courtroom. The Reds mirrored them on the other side. Nazeya, who had not been arrested, was in amongst the crowd—whatever happened, at least *she* was safe.

"I don't like this," Artagne whispered. "This is so bad."

"There's no fucking way this is going to work," Talsyn said.

Saba was inclined to agree. She had lain awake every night since Yermekov had come to parlay. Every night, she came to the same conclusion: The only thing to do was fall and hope the wind caught them. "We came this far. Might as well give it a shot, right?"

"This is so bad," Artagne moaned.

The judge entered, and the room went silent. He climbed the steps to his seat on the platform in the center of the room, and the two clerics following behind—one of Brassu, one of

Mategat—set silver censers on each corner of the barrier and lit knuckle-sized lumps of incense, murmuring prayers and blessings for clarity and wisdom.

Saba's heart beat faster. Her palms were sweating.

With a jolt, she put a name to the feeling: Stage fright. She had stage fright.

Unbelievable. She was *Sabajan fucking Hollant*. Sabajan fucking Hollant did not *get* stage fright.

She straightened her back and looked over at the Reds. Yermekov met her eyes. Saba gave her the tiniest nod, and when Yermekov nodded back, Saba felt it: A breath of wind catching under her wings.

"The trial commences," announced the judge. "The charges laid out are as follows:

"Against Sabajan Hollant: Trespassing, arson, theft, disrupting the public peace and safety. These charges are brought by the Red Theater Players, formerly known as the Lord Seneschal's Women.

"Against Alvana Stillgrail: Trespassing, breaking and entering, attempted theft. These charges are brought by Zitka Yermekov.

"Against the Red Theater Players: Public duelling, trespass, attempted murder, theft, disrupting the public peace. These charges are brought by the Theater of Lights Players, formerly known as the Lord Chancellor's Players. I will hear opening remarks."

Yermekov glanced at Saba again and rose. "Your honor, I would like to speak."

"Mistress Yermekov, I will hear you."

"Thank you."

Yermekov paused.

It was a glorious pause. Not a heartbeat too long or too short. Saba thrilled with it. If only she could teach her newcomers to pause like that.

"I speak for myself and on behalf of my troupe," Yermekov said. "We withdraw all accusations against Sabajan Hollant and the Lights." As the courtroom burst into whispered incredulity, Saba glimpsed a flicker of uncertainty in Yermekov's face—uncertainty, or perhaps stage fright.

"Silence, please," the judge said.

"Silence!" the clerics echoed. Their voices boomed off the rafters, and the crowd settled back down.

For a split second, Saba considered betraying the pact. She could grab at all she ever wanted if she stayed quiet now, if she let Yermekov fall.

Except... that wasn't right, was it? That wasn't everything she wanted—she wanted her theater and her career, certainly. But... she also wanted to be able to live with herself for the next fifty years.

And then there was Nazeya, who had looked up in shock when Yermekov spoke, who was looking back and forth between the two of them.

Saba levered herself out of the chair. "I will speak, your honor," she said.

"Mistress Hollant," the judge said, a little suspicious. "I will hear you."

"I speak for myself and—" Her voice cracked. Her mouth was dry. She swallowed and tried again: "I speak for myself and on behalf of my troupe."

All was silent. She indulged in a glorious pause.

Then, projecting her voice clear to the back of the hall: "We withdraw all accusations against the Red Theater Players."

The judge stared at both of them. "Mistress Hollant, I believe you were imprisoned during the unfortunate incident at the Theater of Lights?"

Saba had negotiated with too many tricksters onstage to

fall for that. 'I was in jail four days ago, your honor, if that is the time you refer to."

'Your rivals ran into your theater brandishing weapons, yet you withdraw charges?"

'I wouldn't call them weapons, your honor."

'Oh no? And what would you call them, Mistress Hollant?"

'Props, your honor."

He furrowed his brows, clearly thrown. 'Props?"

'Yes. You know, fakes. It was just stage fighting."

The judge flipped through some papers on the table in front of him. 'Stage fighting, you say," he muttered, then tapped his finger on something. 'One of your number was gravely injured. It is still uncertain whether she will recover."

'Yes, sir. Terrible, but an accident. Even without using live steel, they do happen."

'And you, Mistress Yermekov? Your theater was burned to cinders."

'Also an accident, your honor," Yermekov said promptly. 'Last night I remembered suddenly that I'd left a lamp burning. My accusation against Mistress Hollant was in error, and I apologize."

The judge narrowed his eyes. 'And what of your troupes? Do they agree that you both speak as their representatives? I warn you, I only need one accuser in order to have a trial."

The two troops slowly got to their feet—every Red. Every Light.

There should have been a swell of music from a quartet of musicians in a balcony above the stage. Saba felt waves and waves of chills go down her spine, imagining it. It wasn't right that this was happening in silence.

The Lights looked at Saba; the Reds, at Yermekov. One by one, slowly at first and then with rising assurance, every last one of them declared to the court that Sabajan Hollant and Zitka Yermekov did indeed speak for them.

~

"Talesyn's teeth, tongue, and *testicles*," Saba gasped as they burst out the doors of the courthouse. "I need a drink. I need five drinks."

"Pub crawl," said Inneo.

"If you mean I'm going to crawl into one pub and stay there for the rest of the evening, then you're not wrong."

"Saba!" someone cried.

Saba stopped and looked back—Nazeya, running down the courthouse steps towards them, her skirts hitched up in both hands so the fabric caught the breeze and billowed out around her in just the same way Saba's heart did at the sight of her.

"Hello," Saba said, feeling suddenly meek. Nazeya had stopped on the step just above Saba, and that extra height—well, that felt *right*. She always wanted to be looking up at Nazeya.

"Saba, what was that?"

"Oh, ah... You might want to ask Yermekov about it. It was her idea, sort of. But she'll probably say it was yours."

"But *why*?"

Saba shrugged and stuffed her hands into her pockets. "She was tired. I was tired. It was the right thing to do."

"It was *amazing*."

There was a light of something beautiful in Nazeya's eyes. Saba wanted badly to throw herself at her feet and—and *declaim* something.

She ducked her head, smiling. "Ah, it was nothing. Just a bit of theater."

"A splendid performance." Nazeya's voice was full of irresistible warmth.

Saba glanced over her shoulder—the Lights were clustered together, not quite out of earshot and *definitely* watching. "We're going to the Theater of Truth. If you like, you're welcome to join us. All of you, I mean." She steeled herself. "And you can tell Yermekov that I'll negotiate with her if she buys me a drink and gives Alvana's dog back."

"Negotiate?"

Saba nodded, not quite meeting her eyes. "I'm going to offer to share our stage with you, but if we try to do it as two separate troupes, then we'll end up battling over the performance schedule. It'd work better if we just joined up, wouldn't it? So... Yermekov can negotiate with me about the name. But *only* if Alvana gets the dog. Or at least joint custody."

When she glanced up, Nazeya was smiling down at her in quiet amazement, dawning joy, awe.

She would've let herself blush, but she was *Sabajan fucking Hollant*—so she picked up Nazeya's hand, kissed her knuckles, and gave her an elaborate and gallant bow.

Artagne, behind her, sighed, "Oh, *Saba*, stop it," and all Saba's skill as a player couldn't keep back her grin.

ABOUT THE AUTHOR

Alexandra Rowland is the author of *A Conspiracy Of Truths, A Choir Of Lies*, and *A Taste of Gold and Iron* (forthcoming June 2022 from Tor.Com Publishing), as well as a Hugo Award-nominated podcaster, all sternly supervised by their feline quality control manager. They hold a degree in world literature, mythology, and folklore from Truman State University.

Find them and more of their work at their website and sign up for the newsletter to be notified about new releases: www.alexandrarowland.net

Or find them on social media:

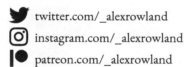

twitter.com/_alexrowland

instagram.com/_alexrowland

patreon.com/_alexrowland